Seventeen Times
As High As The Moon

# Seventeen Times
# As High As The Moon

Short Stories By

## Julia Oliver

*Julia Oliver*

THE BLACK BELT PRESS

Montgomery

This is a work of fiction. The characters, names, incidents, dialogue, and plots are the products of the author's imagination or are used fictitiously. Any resemblance to actual persons or events is purely coincidental.

"Futures" and "Fantasizing" were published in *Southern Humanities Review*. "Conversation" first appeared in *Ascent*. Earlier versions of "Last Respects" and "Saints" appeared in *The Chattahoochee Review* and *The Jefferson Review*, respectively. "Harmonious Arrangement" first appeared in *Brontë Street*. "The Ritual" received the first place award for short fiction in the Deep South Writers' Competition, 1986, and appeared in *Amaryllis*. "Penolia" was a finalist in the PEN/ Syndicated Fiction Awards of 1991. "Mourning" was published in *The Eclectic Observer*. "Heart Pine" first appeared in *Wind Magazine*.

*Design by Randall Williams*

Library of Congress Cataloging-in-Publication Data

Oliver, Julia.
      Seventeen times as high as the moon, and other
      stories / by Julia Oliver.
         p. cm.
      ISBN 1-881320-04-9 : $18.00
      I. Title.
PS3565.L477S46 1992
813' .54—dc20

                                       92-37457
                                         CIP

*For Tommy*

# Contents

# Seventeen Times
# As High As The Moon

# Futures

They arrived at Hargett Farms—the name was painted in forthright letters on a sign where the cross-rail fence began—just past dusk. Mrs. Hargett had prepared what she called her "company supper": a baked ham, studded with cloves and pineapple rings; a spongy casserole known, at least to the Hargetts, as spoon bread; pickled green tomatoes; and tiny pinwheels of sliced okra, fried in cornmeal.

At the table, Marcia said to her friend Katherine, "You can see why I don't come home more often. And you'd better save room for the pecan pie, or you'll hurt Daddy's feelings." The Hargetts weren't run-of-the-mill farmers. They had acres of pecan orchards as well as what Mr. Hargett referred to as his broiler crop—hundreds of chickens, bred scientifically to plump maturity before they were crated up and trucked off to be slaughtered. An air of prosperity, of industry rewarded, hung over the place. The house was spacious and cheerful, with chintz slipcovers on the chairs and sofas, braided rugs on polished oak floors. The scents of grass and animals wafted in through tall, open windows and mingled with the sensuous aroma of food.

Katherine gazed at the sorrowfully beautiful deer's head mounted on the wall across from where she sat. She was feeling somewhat stuffed herself, and caught up in the overflow of affection that was passed around the table almost as tangibly as the silver biscuit box: it was as if Mrs. Hargett had said, "Here, dear, have some."

The drive had taken most of the afternoon, but Katherine was glad she'd accepted Marcia's spur-of-the-moment invitation. If she hadn't been unhappy about how things were going with Ted, she wouldn't have left, even for a week-end.

"Lord knows, we don't have much to offer in the way of diversion around here. They say people come to her from Mississippi, Georgia, and Tennessee. On a good day there might be ten cars in the yard at one time, some of them Cadillacs. And she still charges two dollars, same as she has for years." Mrs. Hargett was a pretty woman, flushed with the victory of her well-received supper, the remains of which coated her best china. Splotched with lipstick and sauces, damask napkins lay in wadded lumps, like wounded birds, beside the plates. Stringy puddles of candle wax collected on the tablecloth. Mrs. Hargett presided over the ruins with unconcerned aplomb. She was trying to persuade the girls to visit the local fortune teller. "I'm not a real believer in such stuff, but other people swear by her. You know Eunice Cousins, Marcia—"

"Indeed I do, Mom. I grew up around these parts, remember?" Marcia's sarcasm was light, bantering. Katherine knew she was rather proud of her mother's giddy provincialism.

Mrs. Hargett, unperturbed, continued. "Well, not long ago, Eunice lost her double strand pearl necklace. I'd have figured the help stole it, but Mrs. Creel told Eunice to look in a certain drawer—not a place she ever would have thought of herself—and sure enough, there it was."

"Somebody could write a book of stories about what that woman's foretold. My favorite," Mr. Hargett said in his booming voice that cut through the cigar smoke surrounding him, "is when she warned everybody a tornado was going to hit town. Bob Snipes"—he inclined his head toward Katherine—"Bob's president of the bank and normally pretty sensible, but soon's he heard the prediction, he chained his brand new car to the biggest tree he could find, to keep it from being blowed clean away—"

Mrs. Hargett interrupted: "Sugar, I think you mean 'blew clean away,' don't you?"

"Let's make it 'blown clean away,'" Marcia said.

"Well, you two have ruined my story I was telling for the benefit of this little lady. Anyway, Mrs. Creel was dead wrong that time; the tornado didn't come, and Bob was made to look like a fool." Mr. Hargett re-inserted the cigar firmly between his teeth.

"Of course, she hardly ever misses," Mr. Hargett resumed huffily, as though he were speaking of himself, "and she doesn't apologize when she does. Just says the spirit wasn't on her at the moment. First time she ever had a vision, she was only two or three years old. She 'saw' her daddy's cows loose in a field which wasn't within sighting distance of the house. When they went to check, the fence was down and those cows were high-tailing it to the road. From then on, she'd get these notions of things about to happen, and most times they did. Before she married she was already set up in what she calls the futures business."

"Futures?" Katherine prompted.

"She won't call it fortune telling, since she's not a gypsy. Mrs. Creel's an institution around here, all right." Mr. Hargett drummed his fingers on the table. Katherine thought he was losing interest in the subject, as was she.

But Marcia wasn't. "I went to her with a bunch of kids when I was thirteen. All I remember about that time is that I took your car, Mom, and of course I didn't have a driver's license, so I probably never told you about it."

"Well, don't tell me now. Marcia was into mischief from the time she started to school until she left for college," Mrs. Hargett explained with obvious pride. Mr. Hargett frowned and cleared his throat; Marcia rolled her eyes.

Katherine stood, aware that she was being rude to initiate the ending of the ritual meal, and picked up her plate. "Everything was delicious. I want to help clean up," she murmured, trying to sound as Southern and gracious as Marcia's mother, and realizing she didn't.

"Oh, no, dear. You need a rest from all that partying and studying you do at the University. I'll just stack things on the kitchen counter for Flora to take care of in the morning." Mrs. Hargett waved her hand in an arabesque over the clutter. Katherine almost expected to see the chaos disappear. She obediently put the plate back on the table. More than anything, she wanted to go to bed. She'd have a room to herself. No Marcia, talking to her in the dark from a few feet away; no Ted, throwing a sweaty arm across her as they lay doubled-up in his single bed. No Ted. Would her life be lopsided without him, if and when it came to that?

"We could go into town for a beer, and check out the local guys," Marcia said after they left the dining room.

"If it's okay with you, I'd rather check out that feather bed your mom showed me," Katherine said.

Marcia yawned. "That sounds good. I wasn't really serious about the guys . . . although I do have this concern that here I am a senior in college, with no husband in sight. I know that's an archaic mindset, but look at my early conditioning. I used to think I couldn't wait to get out of the country, but now, whenever I come back to the land of my six generational roots, it occurs to me that I wouldn't mind spending the rest of my life around here. Do you think that's weird?" Marcia was turning down the bedspread and top sheet on the guest room bed.

"Not in the least." Merely incomprehensible.

Marcia smiled. "You don't care where you end up as long as it's with Ted."

"It's not that simple," Katherine said. It wasn't simple at all, and she didn't want to talk about it. She was very tired, and she wanted Marcia to leave her alone in the pretty room with roses on the wallpaper.

"Right. I forgot. With you two, careers come first. See you in the morning." Marcia gave Katherine a brief hug. Katherine felt their breasts touch through the layers of clothing; comfort without passion. She would miss Marcia. This time next year, Katherine would be in the law school that made her the best scholarship offer. After graduation, Marcia planned to study dance in New York for a few weeks, but by summer's end she'd be back in the warm pit of family. Katherine had a sudden vision of Marcia pirouetting under arched branches of pecan trees that grew in rows as structured as a symphony.

The upstairs windows were thinly curtained. Having slept well, Katherine welcomed the sunshine that bounced into the room early the next morning. The day's plans were laid out at breakfast. Now, in the serenity of a Saturday morning with no tests to study for, no papers to write, they were going to consult Mrs. Creel.

The narrow, unpaved road was surprisingly smooth, but the scenery, viewed from Marcia's Corvette, was depressing. The pastoral perfection of the Hargett lands had given way to a seemingly endless stretch of barren fields that looked, to Katherine, like territory abandoned, or never claimed. Weathered shacks punctuated the landscape as though they were distance markers. Occasionally an old, rusting person, or a clump of children, would stare at the road from a front porch.

Katherine said, "Are we in a time warp?"

Marcia laughed. "Nope, just miles off the main highway, where in this county, things haven't changed much in a hundred years."

"Did you go to school with children who came from these places?"

"Sure, before I went away to boarding school. It upset me that they were barefoot even in the winter, but Daddy said I'd have to get used to it, because we couldn't buy shoes for all of them," Marcia said defensively. "The Creel homestead will be different."

She was right. The small house was painted a fresh lime green, a startling clash with the dark-leafed oaks in the yard. On the front porch, in a high backed rocking chair, was an old man in clean, ironed overalls. "That's her husband," Marcia said.

"Evening," he said as they came up the steps, although it was morning. Marcia made the introductions and asked to see Mrs. Creel.

"A while ago she said she hoped nobody'd stop today, cause she wasn't in the mood. She gets that way. I'll go see will she change her mind." He arose and lumbered into the house. The screen door creaked shut behind him. A bantam rooster appeared from beneath the porch, his curve of tail feathers exquisitely iridescent in the sunshine. Katherine watched the rooster until his black eye met her gaze, then she willed him never to be trapped inside a crate.

Mr. Creel reappeared, followed by a woman who looked enough like him to be his twin. Katherine was disappointed that the woman didn't exude some air of mystery. Mrs. Creel wore tobacco-colored felt bedroom slippers, stenciled with faint outlines of Indian faces, and heavy cotton stockings. Her sparse hair was pulled taut from her forehead and skeined into a tight ball on the top of her head. Her face fell into the hollows of the skull beneath it. She spat an arc of tobacco juice across the porch railing and squinted at each of them briefly before she spoke. "Which one of you wants to start?"

"The driver goes first," Katherine said. She watched as Marcia, glossy as a photograph in her crisp white jeans and pink sweater, entered the dark depths of the house. Katherine sat on the porch railing. The silence felt alien, and she suspected that the old man wouldn't say a word unless prodded, so she said, "How many people does your wife see in a typical day?"

He had resumed rocking; the chair moved back and forth a couple of times before he answered. "Depends. Usually Saturday's real busy, but so far you girls are the only ones been by today."

"I'll bet you have some stories to tell about the people who come here."

"Nope. I don't know who they are or where they come from unless I study the license plates."

She persisted: "Do some look disappointed when they leave—over what she's told them?"

"Never paid much attention. Come to think of it, though, the most disappointed looking of anybody I recall was a man she didn't even talk to. One day a few years back, she took close to thirty folks, one right after the other. Cars were lined up back to the main road there. Finally she came out and told me she couldn't read no more futures that day, 'cause the headache had come on her. She'd taken care of everybody but one young fellow who'd been standing out under that tree for the longest time. I told her to take him 'fore she quit, but she looked out where he was and said, 'He ain't got a future. He'll be dead inside a week.'" Mr. Creel paused to swat at a large-winged insect with his hand. "Course I didn't tell him that. I just told him she had to close up shop for the day, and he was mighty disappointed, but he trudged on off. He'd walked from somewhere, didn't have a car."

"And did he die within the week?" Katherine asked.

"Don't rightly know if he did or not. I never saw him before or since."

"Can she tell your future?"

"No sirree she can't, cause I won't let her. My future belongs to me. She can't read her own, either. She spends nearly every nickel she makes on doctors and chiropractors; if she could tell what was in store for her, she wouldn't have to go to them so much, would she?"

Katherine didn't attempt an answer. She was thinking that she would choke in all that vast silence, if she had to live in such a place.

When Marcia came out, the woman beckoned silently to Katherine from the doorway. "Your turn," Marcia said, avoiding Katherine's eyes.

In the plain room, almost devoid of furniture, Mrs. Creel looked different: authoritative, and more like a seeress. With a bent spoon, she vigorously stirred some wet coffee grounds around in a cup. Then she leaned across the card table and said, almost coyly: "Now, are you really a college girl, or are you playing a trick on me, hiding your wedding ring? Expect me to find out for myself that you're just dying to know whether your baby will be a boy or a girl?"

Katherine laughed in disbelief. "What do your coffee

grounds say about me?"

Mrs. Creel frowned and stared at her for a moment, narrowing her eyes. Then she looked into the cup and said, "They say your big dream is to get married and settle down. You're worried that you haven't met the right man yet, but he's out there, looking for you, too. Don't get impatient. You'll find each other." She stirred the coffee grounds again. "I see three children, a fancy station wagon, and a two-story house with a swimming pool." The woman put the cup down on the table; the gesture, in its finality, was one of tremendous weariness. She said, with evident indifference, "You can ask me something, if you want to, and I'll answer as best I can."

Katherine asked, "Where does it come from? What tells you when someone is going to die, or where to find a lost possession?"

Mrs. Creel raised both arms to fasten a large wire hairpin more firmly into her knot of hair. "You don't believe," she said.

"I could believe, but not in something in the bottom of a cup."

Mrs. Creel shrugged. "Soon as I saw you and your friend, I felt powerful vibrations. I know I didn't hit you right just now. But what I told the other girl had come through to me easy as sucking lemonade through a straw; times like that I know I'm onto the real thing. Sometimes I don't get no vibrations at all, and that could mean the person doesn't have much future, but on the other hand, it could mean I'm just not connecting. Most likely, that's what it means. 'Cause death, when it's close by, is something I see." The woman stood, turned her back to Katherine and gazed out the window. "That's always a burden on me, too."

Marcia had left the fee for both of them with Mr. Creel. In the car, headed back to the main road, she said, "So what did she tell you?"

"The standard traditional stuff—marriage, babies, big house, swimming pool, and station wagon," Katherine said. "No mention of law school or career."

Marcia said, "She told me I was involved with the wrong man, and if I didn't stop sinning, I might end up pregnant, without a husband." She sighed. "As you know, I'm not involved at the moment. I tried to tell her she was way off, but she was adamant. She said she knew what was going on in my life before she even took me into the house."

Katherine saw tears on Marcia's eyelashes. "She got our vibrations mixed up," she said. "She was warning you about what could be my future, and reassuring me about what could be yours."

"Well, I'll buy that," Marcia said. She turned on the car radio. Music filled the space around them and floated off through the sun roof. Katherine hoped some of it would land on those desolate front porches. She glanced sideways at Marcia's profile, which looked clean and young and somehow permanent, like something etched on a coin. Marcia would see to it that they kept in touch. There would be phone calls, letters, Christmas cards through the years; Katherine would be godmother to Marcia's first baby. Ted would disappear in the distance between his medical school and Katherine's law school. He would become an important memory, a scrapbook picture of her youth. These truths arranged themselves in sudden clarity, like playing cards on a table, and she felt them settle into her consciousness as matters already decided upon. But her future, like Mr. Creel's, was her own.

As she watched Marcia's hands beat time on the steering wheel with the music, Katherine began to identify with the rhythm herself. The stalemate was dissolving; something had begun, or maybe something bottled up had been released. She breathed a sigh of relief, and wondered if it was the start of some new happiness.

# Last Respects

The Golden Glade Mortuary was imposing. Elizabeth saw immediately that it was intended to be yet another rendition of Tara; Atlanta would never get over *Gone With The Wind*. She climbed the steps, crossed the flagstone floor of the columned portico, and took a deep breath before she committed herself beyond the massive double doors. Carriage lanterns on either side of the entrance flickered with eternal gas flames.

The place seemed too pretentious even for Simon, but he would have left written instructions as to which funeral home he preferred, in the event he didn't prove to be immortal. In the twenty year duration of their marriage, she couldn't recall that he had ever mentioned the possibility of his dying.

Elizabeth had driven the hundred miles to Atlanta not knowing exactly what was expected of her, the ex-wife, who had left him five years before in proceedings of such complete severance that she'd not seen him since.

She hadn't been able to get back to sleep after the phone call from Simon's sister Beryl had wakened her late the night before. Now here she was, much too soon—hours before the scheduled service—but it didn't seem right to spend the extra time shopping. (Since moving back to her native county, she had missed, more than anything else, Atlanta's wonderful stores.)

Beryl hadn't said anything specific about the arrangements. Had Simon owned a cemetery lot? If so, it hadn't been listed in the property disclosure Elizabeth's lawyer had requested of him. She was surprised that her former sister-in-law called to tell her of Simon's demise. Beryl blamed Elizabeth for the break-up of the marriage, but the fact was that Simon had agreed to the divorce as though it were no matter of great concern to him one way or the other. "If you'd just had children," Beryl had sobbed over the phone, "he wouldn't have died so abandoned!"

Elizabeth let that pass, because she was stunned herself over the news. Simon, who drank in moderation, never used any form of tobacco, walked thirty minutes daily on the treadmill, and kept his weight at 170—Simon had died of a heart attack. Beryl had not spared her the details. He had managed to call the paramedics, who expected from the sounds of background music to find something going on, but it was only Wagner on the compact disc player; Simon was very much alone, slumped over in his leather wing chair. He was wearing a dark red smoking jacket over his pajamas. Elizabeth knew the jacket; on anyone else it would have looked like the start of a Santa Claus costume, but on Simon, well, it was elegant.

Elizabeth removed her gloves, which she had deemed appropriate for the occasion. She looked at her reflection in a pier mirror just inside the foyer. Her slip was showing, just a fraction, and Simon would have found that irritating, but he would have approved of the added touch of the gloves. She was considering putting them back on when she heard a discreet cough, the kind that was supposed to get attention. She turned to see an elderly black man, trimly outfitted in a royal blue uniform complete with brass buttons, gilt braid, and fringed epaulets. His white sideburns were a wonderful added touch; Elizabeth wished she could tell him so, but it didn't seem the time or place.

"Good morning, ma'am," he said. "Are you here to pay respects?"

Elizabeth hesitated, but only for a second, before she gamely replied, "If that's what I'm supposed to do."

"What is the name of your departed?"

"Jackson. Simon Jackson." She almost added, "But I was the one who departed. He stayed where he was, *just* as he was—"

"Please wait here," the man said, gliding away.

Another man, in a much less impressive uniform, plugged in a vacuum cleaner at the far end of the foyer. Piano music—"*Clair de lune*"—commenced from behind a tiered arrangement of potted palms in the curve of the staircase. She expected to see someone seated at a Steinway until she glimpsed the corner of a speaker through the fronds. Simon would have preferred a Bach chorale, something majestic you could beat your breast or gnash your teeth to: "O Sacred Head Now Wounded." But Elizabeth, who worked part-time in a public relations office, approved of the Golden Glade Mortuary's choice of non-jolting Debussy. Mood setting would be important in this business.

The man returned. "Mr. Jackson is in 3-B on the upper level. Are you familiar with our visitation procedure?"

"Well, no," Elizabeth admitted. She wasn't much on making condolence calls at funeral homes; in fact, she couldn't recall having been inside one before. Every funeral she'd attended had started from a church.

She climbed the circular staircase behind her guide to the next floor, where he led her down a carpeted hallway. He stopped at the third doorway and touched her elbow gently. "You may take a seat here to pay your respects. Visitation is limited to forty-five minutes. Please don't go into the roped-off area, that's against our rules." He bowed and moved noiselessly away, leaving her in the doorway of a tiny alcove with a few spindly, straight-backed chairs.

The roped-off area beyond the alcove was a simu-
lated bedroom with glossy reproductions of Victorian
furniture. The poster bed was festooned with a filmy
canopy; a dim, hazy light was provided by electrified
candlesticks on the bedside tables and oh, God, on the
bed was Simon. Attired in a dark suit and centered on
the lavender satin counterpane, his profile all but ob-
scured by a spray of yellow roses, her former husband
now seemed nothing more than conjuration; a surreal,
haphazard mixture of her own memories.

She sat on the edge of a chair, glad she was alone.
Beryl and the others probably would not arrive until
near the time of the funeral. It occurred to Elizabeth
that she could skip that event now that she had come
early to pay her respects. She always had respected
Simon, even when she was most exasperated with him.
Although he was pompous, and affected, and got on her
nerves, in retrospect she could fully appreciate him for
what he was, which was an anachronism. He would
have been happier in the nineteenth century. She was
so glad to be free of him, once the papers were signed,
that she had fled —as though Simon posed a physical
threat to her, which, of course, he never would have.
The move had turned out to be right for her.

Simon, however, would never have moved will-
ingly from the South's foremost cultural enrichment
center (his favorite appellation for Atlanta). Not that

he attended that many concerts, gallery shows, and plays, but he wanted to have them readily available. It was amazing, really, that in the five years since the divorce they hadn't run into each other; she did return to the city from time to time.

Elizabeth was about to take a cigarette from her purse when she saw the No Smoking wall plaque. She'd smoked half a pack in the car driving over. Simon would have lectured her about that; he had liked wearing a smoking jacket, but that's as far as it went with him. She leaned forward, trying to get a better view. It was just as well, she thought, that the flowers and veiling kept him slightly out of focus. Right after Beryl's call, she had a sudden horrible vision of Simon in one of those filing case cabinets they showed in police morgue scenes on television. She didn't want to be morbid, but she couldn't help being curious. Did he, in death, reflect an unhappiness that had to do with her? Was any of this her fault?

Poor Simon. She did feel remiss; she had owed him something for those years of support—God, the alimony! What would happen—? Then she remembered. According to the terms of the divorce, Simon had a life insurance policy which named her as beneficiary. Her finances were in good order; she'd learned how to maintain some semblance of style on those monthly checks. But a lump sum—she'd be tempted to travel, buy a new car.

Elizabeth wondered if there were other visitors who were at this moment also keeping company with the Golden Glade's newly embalmed, and if so, how they were going about it. She wasn't nervous, but she couldn't remember when she'd been so self-conscious. She inhaled deeply, pretending the mouthful of air was tobacco smoke; that trick usually helped her to relax when she couldn't have the real thing. Of course she didn't have to stay the full forty-five minutes, but she'd come all this way to pay her last respects, so she was going to pay them.

"I may as well say a few things to you, Simon." She spoke in a very low voice. "Despite what Beryl says, that you felt tainted by the stigma of divorce, I don't think you were all that miserable without a wife. You certainly could have remarried, if you'd wanted to; you never changed one iota the whole time I knew you, so if I thought you were attractive when we met, other women would have thought so twenty years later . . . . That was part of the problem, however. Not other women, but the fact that you wouldn't change, wouldn't budge the slightest bit . . ." She had begun to speak in a normal voice. She paused, half expecting that frozen, misty profile behind the roses and the veiled hangings to turn full-face toward her and reply.

The voice, however, spoke from the hallway. "Ma'am, I've brought you to the wrong place. The individual laid out in 3-B is Mr. Philip Jackson, and you wished to visit with Mr. Simon Jackson, didn't you? I didn't realize we had two Mr. Jacksons who died in the same twenty-four hours. Yesterday was a busy time for us." He giggled nervously, then said, firmly, as though she were confused and the mix-up had been her fault, "You come along now, ma'am."

Elizabeth was outraged. "You mean I've been sitting here all this time, talking to someone I never knew?"

"Five minutes, ma'am," the man said. "That's all the time you were here. And I'm really sorry."

They were back in the downstairs foyer; Elizabeth heard her high heels click crisply on the marble floor. She was relieved to be away from the seductive carpeting of the upper level. She was relieved to be away from the upper level, period.

"So where is Simon?" she asked, lighting a cigarette. The man wouldn't dare stop her after the humiliation he'd just caused her.

"Uh—did you say you were kin to him?"

"I didn't say one way or the other," she said. Really!

"This may come as a shock to you, ma'am. The fact is, Mr. Simon Jackson's ashes are being readied now for his memorial service this afternoon." The man backed away from her, watching her face for her reaction.

Elizabeth exhaled a cloud of gray smoke. She coughed, and coughed again. Simon would be reduced to his essence at once, with no changing, no evolving, over a period of time. His ashes would be placed in a handsome bronze urn and relegated to a shelf in Beryl's library. No lawn mowers would run over his grave; he wouldn't be rained on, wouldn't rot. Simon would consider cremation the next best thing to perfect preservation, which, of course, was not an option, even for him.

She was coughing and laughing at the same time.

The black man showed such concern that she rummaged around in her purse and came up with a five dollar bill. As his palm closed over the gratuity, his face registered surprise and hurt. Well, he had on a doorman's uniform, didn't he?

She was gliding along the interstate, her cruise control set at 65, before the laughter subsided. She opened the dashboard ashtray, which was full of snubbed-out butts, tinged with her lipstick, and powdery ash. Even though it was against the law, or environmental rules or something, she rolled down the car window and emptied the contents of the metal container into the wind.

"Good-bye, Simon, old friend," she said, and she felt the sadness begin to suffuse her. She couldn't remember what he looked like. She was afraid she would always see him lying there, his face shrouded in a mist of dim light and veiling, part of some hideous caricature of a fine and noble myth.

# Fantasizing

The supple arm that had spun glittering parabolas with a baton under stadium lights now made energetic swirls with a sponge across a stained Formica counter. She hadn't been there but a couple of weeks. Before that, she had worked in the mall on the other side of town, and he seldom saw her. Now he could spend a few minutes each weekday afternoon in her presence.

Jack inhaled the last of the good stuff from his unfiltered cigarette and broke its spine in the metal ashtray. He was glad the Stop and Sup Cafe hadn't been divided into smoking and non-smoking sections like some larger establishments in town. Smoking went with coffee drinking and was one pleasure he never intended to deny himself. The restaurant was across the street from the mill entrance; it took him a few minutes to get there and back. The other guys didn't cross the street for breaks, only for lunch. But he always met his

wife Alma, who was the mill manager's secretary, in the employees' cafeteria at noon. (Alma turned up her nose at the Stop and Sup.)

"Things dull enough for you, Jack?" Mary Lou gave him a coffee refill and emptied his ashtray. The tiny beads of perspiration on her upper lip didn't repel him.

"Duller than I ever dreamed they could be," Jack answered truthfully. "I can't imagine why we stayed in this town." He dared to link her to him with that "we."

She shrugged, missing the link. "It never occurred to me and Duck to leave."

First semester of their senior year in high school—fourteen years before—Mary Lou had eloped with her boy friend Duck Whatley, the star quarterback on the football team. Duck hadn't amounted to much since. He was still a termite sprayer, hadn't budged from the job he'd got right after graduation. But it didn't give Jack any satisfaction that he and Alma had more going for them, in the way of good positions and company benefits, than Mary Lou and Duck. He would like to be working for the benefit of Mary Lou, even as a termite sprayer.

Jack was the only person sitting at the counter. An old man he didn't know was reading a newspaper in a booth within earshot, but it was as good a time as any to ask her. "You happy with your life, Mary Lou?"

"That's a brain-taxing question." Her eyes clouded like she'd grown cataracts all of a sudden. "I'd say yes

and no. I think I expected something better, but it's not all bad."

"Well. You got a couple of nice kids, I hear." He hadn't heard they were nice; he just knew she had them.

"Shirley Jean is thirteen. Can you believe she'll be old enough to try out for majorette next spring?" Mary Lou's face brightened and her voice moved up a tone. "She's the delight of my life. Little Ralph barely got promoted from fifth grade. He definitely got his daddy's intelligence."

She laughed like she didn't care whether the kid was dumb or not.

"I saw Alma in the beauty parlor last Saturday. She's sure holding her looks, Jack."

What she really meant was that even if Alma wasn't anything special when they were all young, she was coming into her own now. Alma knew how to dress and make the most of herself. So Alma herself told him often enough.

"How come y'all don't adopt a kid? If she hasn't gotten pregnant by now, she's not gonna." Mary Lou took a cigarette from the pack in his shirt pocket. She rested both elbows on the counter as she held it out for him to light. He could have looked clean down the neckline of her uniform, past the shadow where her peach-colored flesh swelled and divided, but he didn't. Fantasizing was enough.

"We've started going to a fertility specialist in Birmingham," Jack said, embarrassed.

"That sounds like somebody who tells you how to rotate crops," Mary Lou said. Her eyes turned cloudy again. "Y'all better not wait too long. I heard they won't let you get a baby after you're a certain age. Believe me, I might not stay with Duck if it weren't for my kids."

"Is Duck mean to you, Mary Lou?" Jack gripped the mug.

"Nah, he's not mean. It's just that we don't have anything to say to each other except whatever's going on with the kids. If Shirley Jean makes majorette, that'll give us something to look forward to. You know, we can talk a lot about that." She had come around and perched on the stool next to him. He could smell the fruity, metallic scent of her: a mixture of starched uniform, hair spray, and cosmetics. She took an emery board from the pocket of her uniform and fiddled it across a ruby-colored thumbnail.

"What can I do for you, Mary Lou?" His voice trembled with the weight of his offering.

"Well, let's see. Like you just said, it's pretty dull around town nowadays. You could whip us up a little excitement." She regarded him sideways. "You always used to be good for livening things up, Jack. I'll never forget the time, senior year, that you jumped in that police car and drove it out on the field at the half—when your knee was hurt and you couldn't play."

"Miracle I didn't get kicked out of school for that," he said, hoping she didn't see how pleased he was that she remembered the incident. The only reason he'd done it was to capture her attention; at the time he hadn't known that he had succeeded. The week after it happened, Mary Lou and Duck cut classes one day to get married and came back to school the next. But she quit school at Thanksgiving, right after the last game— she was pregnant, and by then she'd begun to show.

"What a thrill that was, seeing you hanging out the window, driving around in crazy circles all over the field with the siren going," she said softly.

"They'd put me under the jail if I did something like that now." Jack looked at his watch. Just when the conversation was really taking off, he had to get back to work. He folded a dollar bill under the saucer so the man in the booth wouldn't see he'd tipped too much.

Mary Lou said, "Y'all ought to come to the game tonight. We're going. I'll give Shirley Jean some pointers while the band's performing at halftime. Of course Duck will spend the whole game bragging to Little Ralph about the way he used to play." She went back behind the counter to the cash register to ring up his fifty cents for the coffee. She smiled to show she'd spotted the corner of the dollar bill sticking out under the saucer.

"I'd rather go to a movie," Alma said. Jack was

bringing in the last sack of groceries. On Fridays they stopped at the discount super market on the way home from work to stock up with microwave dinners. Alma was a career person, which entitled her not to cook.

"It's first home game of the season," Jack said. "When I was on the team, we got a big boost from a good turnout in the stands to watch us. We'd look up at all those folks and we'd think we could do just about anything—"

"Well, you couldn't, if I remember correctly. You rode out most of your time on the bench until you busted your knee playing football on that field. We haven't been to any games in the last couple of years. Why start going again now?" Alma never had liked football, although she'd played clarinet in the same high school band that Mary Lou, in her short skirt, fringed boots and glory, had strutted in front of.

"I want to go tonight," Jack said, surprising both of them with his stubbornness.

Alma sighed. "All right," she said, as though the ultimate decision was hers alone, "We'll go this time."

Alma had brought cushions for them to use on the hard backless seats of the open bleachers. People sat in isolated clusters, like birds on a fence. "I wouldn't say high school football is exactly the big event in this town it used to be," she said. "Bet you anything half the town is out at the mall right now. See, most folks don't feel the need to support the team."

Jack didn't answer. He had spotted Mary Lou and her family seated on the top row above the band right about the fifty yard line. Alma had already chosen their seats, low on the thirty. She didn't like heights and she wanted to be near the exit. He wouldn't be able to watch Mary Lou, but she could see the back of his head, where his hair was beginning to thin, if she happened to look that way.

Right in his line of vision was a blue and white police car, turreted on top with a big dome light, parked by the field entrance. A couple of uniformed cops were standing, arms folded, near the bench of the visiting team. Jack couldn't recall that there'd ever been a real riot at one of the high school games, but every now and then tempers flared and a fight started. That's why policemen, with their powerful official vehicle, were on hand. Which is how he nearly got into bad trouble. It had been a sudden impulse, not even something done on a dare: unobserved, he had hobbled into the driver's seat, tossed his crutches into the back, started the engine—the keys had been left in the ignition—and gunned the big sedan onto the field. In the first brief seconds he even figured out how to activate the siren. Mary Lou had screamed with laughter when he brought the car to a screeching halt right in front of where she waited, with the other majorettes, to begin the band's halftime exhibition. Just as clearly, he remembered the aftermath, especially being taken in the same car to the police station. He said to Alma: "Do you remember when I drove the police car out on the field during a game?"

She unwrapped a stick of gum and folded it neatly before popping it into her mouth. "Not if I can help it," she said. "I was so horrified for you. You could have ruined your whole future."

"It's not the only stupid thing I've ever done."

"No, it's not. But it's certainly the most stupid thing you've done so far."

Actually, Jack thought, it wasn't. The most stupid thing had been marrying Alma.

When the home team made a touchdown in the first quarter, the skimpy crowd roared almost in unison, but Jack thought he could pick out Mary Lou's voice from the chorus. Alma said, when the cheering subsided, "It's obvious this is going to be a one-sided game. If we leave now, we can still catch the second show."

"I'm staying. But right now I'm going to the john," he said. To keep her from coming with him, he added, "I'll bring you a hot dog. What you want to drink?"

"Diet Pepsi. Make sure it's Diet, too," she said. She glared at him as though he'd said something to insult her.

Mary Lou came up to him at the concession stand. She had her daughter with her. "We didn't eat supper, so I thought I'd beat the halftime crowd here to get us some food. Anyway, at the half I got to be watching the majorettes. Jack, this is Shirley Jean. Hon, this man here and I went all through high school together."

With small sharp features and a few scattered pimples on her face, the girl looked more like Duck than she did her mother.

"I hear you're going to try out for majorette yourself this spring," he said.

Shirley Jean scowled and jerked her head in her mother's direction. "She wants me to. I'd rather be a cheerleader."

"Either way, you'll be great," Jack said. He had not allowed himself the pleasure of switching his gaze to Mary Lou.

"What d'you say?" Mary Lou nudged her daughter with her elbow.

"Thanks," Shirley Jean said, without enthusiasm. "I'm going to the ladies', Mom. Get me a hamburger."

"Get me a hamburger, *please*," Mary Lou said, but the girl had dashed off. She sighed. "I try to work on her manners. It's a hard age. At least she hasn't got fat like some girls in her class."

"She's a very attractive young lady," Jack said. "But she'll have a long way to go to catch up with her mama." He felt his face flush, wondering whether he'd said the wrong thing.

"Hey. That's a nice compliment. Thanks."

"Okay. You're welcome."

They procured cardboard trays with wrapped up food and drinks in cartons. Mary Lou got hers first, waving away his attempt to pay. "You got no cause to feed my family," she said.

They walked away from the concession stand together and were level with the police car when Mary Lou said, "That's parked right about where the one you stole was, isn't it?"

"Borrowed, not stole," Jack said. "Same spot. That one was a Ford. Now they got Chevys." He bent and looked inside the open window on the driver's side. The keys were in it; he had known they would be. Policemen always left keys in the cars in case they had to make quick getaways.

Mary Lou sucked in her breath. "Think you could pull it off again? Like right now?"

"I didn't pull it off back then," Jack said. "And it wouldn't be funny this time. Besides, it's not halftime yet. Field's not empty."

"Yeah. And it wouldn't solve anything. It wouldn't bring anything back," she said. She moved away from the car.

"What's to bring back?" Jack was genuinely puzzled. Had she, in fact, had some feeling for him back then he'd never known about?

"You know . . . the good times," she said. "High school was the very best time of my life. I was so crazy about Duck, and when I watched him throw those long passes, or tossed my baton fifteen feet up in the air and caught it without a hitch—it was like we could do absolutely anything we wanted to. And then when you got in that car and set the siren going and careened all around the field ahead of the band, that kind of summed it up. It was like you were making a statement for all of us: See, we can do anything."

"That's not why I drove the damn police car," Jack said. "High school wasn't the best time of my life."

Mary Lou looked at him as if he'd said something obscene. They were walking behind the end zone bleachers to get back to their side. There was plenty of time for Jack to get the words right in his mind to tell her, even if she didn't want to hear the real reason why he'd done such a crazy thing. He had his mouth open to begin, not at all sure that it would come out like he wanted it, when the crowd started yelling again.

"We scored another touchdown!" Mary Lou almost dropped her cardboard tray in her excitement. "Jack, we did it again! We're still the greatest!" Her face lit up like the moon had landed on it.

She ran nimbly ahead of him. By the time he got to the bleachers, she was already up on the top row with her children and her husband. Duck never even glanced at her as she handed him his food. Jack gave Alma her hot dog and drink. "It's Diet Pepsi," he said, before she could ask him.

The game was seventeen to nothing at the half.

Jack told Alma he'd just as soon leave. The band was beginning its fast march onto the field, led by drum rolls and a row of majorettes in short skirts, their still-suntanned legs flashing a last bit of summer into the autumn night.

Jack didn't look back as the cornets and trombones lurched into the first thumping strains of the Sousa. He knew that Mary Lou, with her uninterested daughter, would be watching quicksilver arcs of batons thrown skyward.

"You're right," he conceded to Alma. "Football in this town isn't at all the big event it used to be."

She smiled at him with relief and a certain tenderness, as though they had just ended a long, unnecessary argument.

# Epiphany

Mary Beth and her housekeeper got on extremely well, and had for thirty-five years. During the tense times of the civil rights movement the two women had focused empathy on each other's personal happinesses and heartbreaks; the larger issue loomed like thunderclouds, but beyond the walls of the house.

Never once had Clara intimated that she was in any way unhappy with her life, although her husband had deserted her and the state of Alabama years before. Stoic herself, Mary Beth admired Clara's steadfastness of spirit. So it was with a great deal of surprise that she heard Clara announce, one day toward the end of February, that she wanted to join the Episcopal Church.

"I've been thinking about it for a good while now—ever since Mr. Ben's funeral." Clara talked as she swished the feather duster over the curve of the piano.

Mary Beth took a swallow of tea. "I can't believe

you'd actually leave Mount Zion Baptist."

"I've been dissatisfied for a long time, and not just with the choir director. The real reason I want to make a change is there are things about your service I admire. Such as, the preacher doesn't raise his voice at his flock."

"Sometimes he comes mighty close. You've just been to St. Paul's for the girls' weddings and Ben's funeral and little Kelly's baptism. Those were all special occasions." Mary Beth took the duster from Clara to whisk at a layer of dust on the piano pedals. "Every time you go over the top, you need to make a swipe at the bottom, too."

"I was coming to that place." Clara retrieved the duster and moved on to the bookshelves. "What got me thinking the most was when we were talking about our own funerals a while back. You remember?"

"Vaguely."

"I asked would you come to my service and stand by the preacher and speak some words about me. You said—"

"I remember now. I said I would."

"But when I offered to do the same for you if you died first, you said Episcopalians didn't hold with spontaneous testimonials, and that got me thinking, I wouldn't want just anybody to speak about me at my funeral, and they might."

"I prefer predictability in religious rituals myself.

Not that I'm the kind of Episcopalian you should take for a role model. You know I don't go to church as often as I should." Mary Beth took her cup and saucer back to the kitchen.

Clara followed. "I know you go when you feel the need to, same as me. And last Sunday I felt the need to visit the Church of the Holy Redeemer."

Mary Beth had begun to clean out the refrigerator. She squatted in front of the open door and took out a bowl of tomato aspic. "This has been in here since I had bridge club last week. If you or I don't eat something in three days, for God's sake, Clara, throw it out! Else we'll have food poisoning and simultaneous funerals. In which case neither of us can go to the other's."

"Was a time when you never wanted me to throw anything away, even potatoes that had sprouted."

"You know that's not so. I never have liked clutter." Mary Beth got up and took the aspic to the sink. She turned on the faucet and the garbage disposal.

Clara's voice lifted effortlessly above the noise. "The Holy Redeemer is the colored Episcopal church."

"Black, Clara. No one says colored any more."

"Anyway, I went to the service, and I got up and down at the wrong time once or twice, but I felt in my heart like I belonged. Only thing was, nobody socialized with me after church let out. The main folks who go there are doctors and lawyers and teachers at the colored college."

"Shelbyton College is no longer exclusively for black people."

"Those folks may be richer in worldly goods, but they're still the same color as I am." Clara poured herself a cup of coffee and rendered it almost white with milk.

"All this time you've been drinking coffee and I've been drinking tea, wonder why one of us didn't change? It certainly would have simplified things around here." Mary Beth emptied a carton of buttermilk down the sink.

"How come you wasted that buttermilk? It keeps a long time. I could use it to make biscuits if we decide we want some."

"You and I should each shed twenty pounds. We don't need any biscuits unless the children are coming for a visit, and believe me, they're not anytime soon. They wore us to a frazzle last month when they brought the baby to be baptized, remember?"

"What I mainly remember was that sweet service. I about cried when the preacher sprinkled water on little Kelly."

"So did I . . . . The whole front of the christening gown was soaked, and you'd done such a beautiful job of ironing it." Mary Beth sniffed a head of lettuce. "This may hold up another day or so. Clara, in the Episcopal church the preacher is called the rector. The boys and girls who carry the cross and light the candles are crucifers and acolytes. If you act like you know enough about it, the Holy Redeemer's congregation won't snub you."

"I already figured that out. So, I wondered could I borrow your little book with the holy words—Epiphany, Litany, Pentecost, and such as that? I want to study it."

"Don't take on too much at first. You should just pick one thing to work on, like the Apostles' Creed."

Clara left that afternoon with Mary Beth's black leather prayer book. If Clara decided to go through confirmation, Mary Beth would give her one just like it, with her name stamped in gold on the cover. And that was the extent of her thought on the subject until Clara brought it up again the following Monday.

"I went to the Church of the Holy Redeemer again yesterday," Clara said by way of greeting that morning. "I said the Apostles' Creed without looking at the book. Anybody who looked at me could tell I knew it absolutely by heart."

"Good for you," Mary Beth said over her newspaper. "That's a lot to memorize."

"Those folks still didn't talk to me outside church."

"Did you know anybody there?"

"Dr. Clemmons passed the plate. He's the one gave me my blood pressure prescription after I had that dizzy spell last month."

Mary Beth said, "Do you think maybe your clothes aren't as spiffy as theirs?"

Clara sighed with relief now that the problem was

out. "I wore that dark blue print, your last year's club meeting dress, and had the new shoulder purse you gave me for Christmas, and that nice warm coat you let me have a while back. But every single one of those ladies had on a fur cape or jacket."

"That coat is a classic style, and it's part cashmere. Wool of that quality never wears out." Mary Beth thought for a moment. "The weather's supposed to stay cold for another couple of weeks. Take my fur coat to wear next Sunday."

"You know I couldn't do that," Clara said reprovingly.

"Of course you could. You still have that small black hat with the veiling on it? Wear it, too. Hats like that are coming back in."

The following Monday morning, Clara brought in the ranch mink coat made of matched female pelts (with Mary Beth's full name embroidered like scripture in the lining), and laid it reverently across the back of the living room sofa. She said, "When I came out after the service, several people introduced themselves to me. You see, not one of those ladies had a wrap that hit her past her hips. And here I was, decked out in fur near to my ankles like I was a polar bear."

"Polar bears are white as snow," Mary Beth said.

"Some other kind of bear, then. I thank you from the bottom of my heart for trusting me with it."

"For heaven's sake. I'd trust you with my life." Mary

Beth picked up the coat and felt it ripple in her arms like something alive and alien. It had been her husband's last gift to her, but she was tired of such trappings; why didn't she just give the damn thing to Clara and be done with it? Because, of course, her daughters would think she had lost her mind. She said, with firmness, hoping Clara wasn't aware of her ambivalence: "You know you're welcome to take it again next Sunday."

"Thank you all the same, but it wouldn't be the truth."

"Are you sorry you wore it yesterday, then?"

Clara smiled. "Oh, no. I figure Jesus overlooks a touch of transgression every now and then. I just wouldn't feel right parading myself in your fine fur a second time. Anyway, looks like we're in for an early springtime; our azaleas out back are fixing to bloom. Next Sunday I'll break out my warm weather clothes, maybe that pink, light-weight suit you gave me year before last."

Mary Beth recalled every word of that conversation the next week, when she sat by the hospital bed where Clara lay in a coma, following a massive stroke. Clara had no children, no siblings. Mary Beth assumed that she was the logical person to make the burial arrangements. As Clara was between churches, the service should be graveside. Mary Beth would ask the rector of The Holy Redeemer to conduct the funeral with the understanding that she, too, would speak some words about Clara; if he wouldn't agree to her participation, then she'd have the man from Mount Zion Baptist officiate.

She was thinking through the details while she watched Clara's life dissolve. No one should be weighted down for eternity by a mink coat. She would buy Clara a silk dress as comfortable as a nightgown to be buried in, and she would make a pall of azalea branches for the casket. The backyard bushes were at their peak, a mixture of bud and open bloom. "I believe that's what you would prefer," she leaned forward and said into the empty air around Clara's face.

But the matter of the mink coat was a worrisome thing that would not leave her mind. Clara had said her wearing it was not the truth. Or was it? Mary Beth considered the question from every angle. Finally she found some relief in acknowledging that however temporary it was, an official swap had taken place. Clara had become the owner of the mink coat, while she herself was cocooned, for one epiphanous moment, in the color of Clara's skin.

# Heart Pine

Anne, gouging clumps of weeds from the ghost of a vegetable garden, knelt over her task as if in prayer. Robert, watching from the back door, thought she looked almost appealingly menial, as perhaps women used to look long ago. He didn't want to regard her as being in any way servile. He would prefer that she microwave something for supper, rather than grow it from seed, and fulfill herself creatively otherwise; but she intended to plant and harvest winter greens, whatever those were.

She had begun wearing her hair pulled back in a twisted knot like a pioneer woman. They had lived in the house for less than a month, yet she was convinced it was the home she had always wanted. The week before, while they were involved in minor wrangling over how much the improvements were costing in both time and money, he had reminded her that they were renters with a six-month lease.

"Which provides us with an option to buy, and we could be here a long time. You said so." She had regarded him gravely.

"I don't recall saying that exactly," he evaded. "I'm not sure I'll want to stay on at the college after this year."

"You wanted a teaching schedule that would leave you time for writing, and you have it," she said. "You said yourself that the college has a sound reputation, and the town is both progressive and pleasant."

Anne had often described herself as an Army brat who was never allowed to put down roots anywhere. Robert had grown up in the heart of a big city like a weed in a crack of pavement. He, too, had pined for the permanence of a tranquil, solid place. He had a fresh doctorate and few other credentials except his new wife when he was offered a position on the faculty of a liberal arts college in a small town deep in the South.

They found the sturdy, unpretentious farmhouse, with a "For Sale Or Rent" sign, just outside the city limits. Robert remembered the look on Anne's face when they first went inside. The high-ceilinged, square rooms and the wide hall that ran through the center of the house—dogtrot style, according to the real estate agent—were airy and cool even in August, when they moved in.

Built before the Civil War, the house had been surprisingly well kept. The wiring was adequate, the kitchen wasn't totally antiquated. The out-of-state owner "definitely wants to sell," the real estate agent said, "but he'll rent, if the tenant agrees to do some maintenance."

"Is it haunted?" Anne had whispered. She had gone from room to room walking on tiptoe, as though she would not disturb the silence.

"Not that I've heard," the agent said. "But I do know an interesting story about this place. There's a little building, looks like a dollhouse, right at the end of that crape myrtle hedge behind the barn—you can see it from here." Anne and Robert joined him at the wide kitchen window. "The family that first settled this farm came with two pine boxes which contained the remains of their dead babies. They built that little house to hold those coffins. The story is that the woman meant to take the baby boxes with her, if she ever had to move on again. But the family thrived here, and by the time Sam Hurst and his wife died, they'd left two or three grown children. It's a shame nobody thought to bury those infants' remains with the mother in the old Methodist Church graveyard."

"You mean the coffins are still in the little house?" Robert said.

"Sure are."

Anne said, "She could look out the window every day and keep watch over her departed children."

Robert coughed with embarrassment and said, "I'm

surprised it hasn't rotted through."

"The vines have about covered it again, but that little house has been given a good coat of paint and a new roof every time the big house got 'em, and they're both made of heart pine. Can't beat heart pine for endurance," the agent said. He reiterated that the rent was cheap because the inside maintenance was to be done by the tenant. And, having been vacant for close to a year, the house could use some fixing up.

"Oh, we'll enjoy doing that ourselves," Anne assured him. The fixing up began as soon as they moved in. She made muslin curtains for the downstairs rooms and Robert painted. Together they had waxed the wide-plank floors.

He whistled from the doorway to let her know he was watching. He had begun to worry about her, alone out there, while he was at the college in town, several miles away. And yet the appeal of the house, to him, had been its isolation, as well as its unencumbered space. He had appropriated one of the upstairs rooms for his study. Like an empty box waiting to be filled, the room became a metaphor for the novel he would write in it. Anne had selected one end of the large kitchen for her sewing machine and easel.

He walked to where she crouched, the arc of her back as gently curved as a dove's wing. She looked at him almost without recognition.

"You in a trance with nature?" he said.

"As a matter of fact, I was." She stood, wiping dirt from her hands on an old flour sack apron she was wearing over her jeans. Smudges of black loam were on her face.

"Where'd the apron come from?" Robert frowned. He wasn't altogether fastidious, but he'd never seen Anne quite so disheveled and dirty.

"I found it hanging on a hook in the kitchen pantry. But it's clean—or was, til I wore it around all day. Robert, I'm really happy here."

He changed the subject. "Did you go to the doctor?"

"I called and made an appointment for day after tomorrow," she said. She put one hand on the small of her back and grimaced. "I may have overdone it today. I'm a little sore from bending over."

Robert was instantly solicitous. She was pregnant— the test kit she bought at the drug store had confirmed her condition. The night before, they had celebrated with a bottle of wine and delicatessen sandwiches and candlelight at their new, really old, oak table (found in a local antique shop). The news that he would become a father still lay lightly on his mind, not yet assimilated. Although birth control had been an occasional topic of conversation, he could not recall that they had discussed the matter of when they would start a family. Now it was a fact: a child was launched, planned or not. He glanced up at the second floor of the house where rooms still in need of fresh paint awaited him. The baby would need space, too.

As if reading his thoughts, she said, "I think the corner room over our bedroom would be good for the nursery."

"You mean it could stay up there by itself?" Their bedroom was downstairs on the back of the house, close to both the kitchen and the bathroom that had been installed some years before, with noisy but functional plumbing and a clawfoot tub. Anne assumed a bathroom could be put in upstairs (in the event they did buy the house) when they could afford it.

"Of course we'll keep him or her—don't say 'it'— down with us at first, in a bassinet right by our bed. Maybe we'll come across an old cradle to buy." She had the rapt look that Robert had come to dread.

"We're going to have a modern baby who wears disposable diapers and eats baby food from jars. Don't pretend you're just off a covered wagon when you get ready to birth this infant," he said.

"I was thinking I might use the local midwife, who happens to be our closest neighbor, Belinda Bell. Isn't that a wonderful name? She stopped by today. She told me to ring our big farm bell if I ever need her. They don't have a phone. She's a real old-fashioned, salt-of-the earth woman."

Robert said, "Forget that. We have medical insurance, and I want you to have a bona fide obstetrician."

Anne pulled his head down to hers. As she kissed

him he thought he tasted the rich dark soil, which smelled slightly of compost. Offended, he drew back.

She said, "Robert, don't resist the place so. There's a way of life that comes with this house, like a gift; we can learn it if we just go with the flow."

Robert said, "You actually want to be on best friends status with a woman over twice your age who spends her days hoeing in the fields or delivering babies and who probably didn't get past eighth grade?"

Anne was again on her knees, digging at the weeds with almost savage thrusts of her trowel. As if providing an answer, she said, "You can listen to your tapes and play your cello as loud as you want to; nobody will yell for you to be quiet."

"I'm having the feeling that I've made a mistake. The department is a lot narrower in scope than the interview led me to believe." He felt a surge of power in his petulance, but she smiled at him with an even mixture of tolerance and affection.

She said, "Eventually, you could be head of the department, if you made it a goal." He told her he thought that remark was inappropriate. She knew he liked to teach and write and would leave administration to others.

A few days later, Robert was negotiating with Belinda Bell's son, who appeared to be mildly retarded, to mow the meadow. Anne had wanted him to buy a small tractor and take care of that chore himself; she said he would really get into it—it, he presumed, being that flowing way of life—if he'd just get involved in the outside work. He said he had other uses for his spare time now that the downstairs painting was finished.

But Anne could hardly wait to complete one project before she began a new one. She was edging a large flower bed on one side of the house with a border of crumbly old bricks she'd found neatly stacked in the barn. She thought the bricks could have been left over from the original construction, maybe even slave-made. She also had plans to buy a cow to inhabit the barn. She said the baby, after she stopped nursing of course, would thrive on fresh milk. Belinda would teach them how to milk and care for the cow.

As if he were explaining something to one of his slower students, he said, "You must forget any ideas you have about turning this place into a functioning farm. I've gone along with the stage set—the rag rugs and the iron pots hanging over the stove and even the cat that's taken up with us—but that's as old-homesteady as I'm getting." He was biding his time until he told her he did not want to renew the lease. They could find an apartment in town. He wasn't pleased with the deal he'd made with the Bell boy; keeping the wild grass mowed would be more expensive than he'd expected. Sometimes there was a moment of entering the atmosphere of the place—driving into the thickness of incessant cacophony of birds and insects—that he found particularly oppressive. But Anne would be waiting at the end of the long narrow driveway, and the sight of her (always serene, with a patina of happiness on her face) relieved and reassured him. He had begun to have a fear that he would find her hurt or ill.

As it turned out, something did happen, but he was right there, able to help her. While trying to dislodge a wasp's nest from beneath the eaves with a broom, she fell over the low porch railing. Robert, at work on his novel upstairs, heard her plaintive call through the window. When he reached her, she told him that she wasn't hurt, but a dull, cramping pain had begun in her stomach. "Ring the bell," she said. "Belinda will know what to do."

Obediently, he ran to the tall post in the front yard and took the rough rope in both hands and rang the heavy bell; the noise reverberated down his arms. He thought it sounded like doom. Before Belinda arrived in an ancient truck, Robert had carried Anne inside and called the doctor, whose instructions were to bring her to the hospital.

The only hospital in town was not very large. Robert hoped that the doctor knew his business. Belinda had suggested to him, while he was getting Anne into the car, that she could try to save the baby with a potion of herbs, but Robert had dismissed her almost curtly.

The only other person in the waiting room was a man about his own age who wore overalls and a baseball cap. "Having your first?" the man asked him. Robert nodded. He didn't want to admit that his wife was having a miscarriage.

The man inhaled heavily on his cigarette and his words crowded a curl of smoke from his mouth. "My third," he said, sighing with pride. "My wife had the sonar, and she told doc not to tell her, she wanted to be surprised, but he told me. It's another boy. Course she wanted a girl, we got two boys, but man, if you ask me, I'd take all boys. Few more and I'll have my own baseball team."

The man had left to assist with the birthing of his third son before the doctor, a middle-aged man in a white coat with fresh wine-colored stains (Anne's blood?), reported to Robert. Almost jovially, he said: "She's just fine. This episode won't set her back physically." He paused, looking at Robert as though assessing him. Did he appear to be father material? Robert tried not to slump under the scrutiny. "I'll have the package ready for you when you take her home later this afternoon. Maybe it's not a bad idea, having a little funeral, may help her deal with the loss. Some women suffer real emotional damage because they think they did something to cause miscarriage. Of course that fall precipitated hers, but she might have aborted anyway. I'm still a believer in nature going about correcting mistakes."

"Are you saying there was an abnormality with the fetus?" Robert heard himself blurt the words.

"Not necessarily. Could be this one just wasn't ready to make the commitment." The doctor yawned behind his hand. "If you're really going to have a burial, I'd suggest you stop by Larry Peak's veterinary office on the way home. He sells pet caskets that are pretty near the same as some made for infants, but a lot cheaper." He clapped Robert on the shoulder and shook his hand firmly.

Anne said, quickly, as soon as he saw her, "I told the doctor we want to take the baby with us. I don't want it put in an incinerator like garbage."

"For God's sake, Anne. You were barely two months along. It wasn't a baby, it was a tadpole."

"It was our firstborn," she insisted, with a fierceness that surprised him.

"All right," Robert said humbly. "But it would be easier to forget if you don't force this issue of taking the remains."

"I don't intend to forget," Anne said. "Why should I?"

She did not need a wheel chair to get to the car. They left the hospital with the plastic bag (its contents chilled) inside a paper grocery sack that a nurse thought-fully provided. Anne held the parcel in her lap while he drove; they listened to the car radio and did not talk. The pet casket, of lightweight white plastic that looked as if it were made of marshmallow, was also hidden by brown paper wrapping.

Robert knew exactly what would take place after they got back to the house, although they hadn't discussed it further, except that she thanked him, with tears in her eyes, for obtaining the casket.

She led the way over the worn path across the long stretch of back yard into the edge of the brush. He had taken the casket from its wrappings. He held it while she opened the hinged lid and placed the well-wrapped bundle, which contained the stuff of their conception, inside. The veterinarian's nurse had given him a small tube of sealant; Anne took that from him, too, knowing he did not really want to be involved, and carefully sealed the seam.

He had not so much as glanced at the dwarf mausoleum since the real estate agent showed it to them from the kitchen window. He saw now that someone— Anne, of course—had cleared the vines from its roof and walls. He hung back, unable to offer to help, as she knelt and unlatched the door. A smell as elusive as some long-past season came at his nostrils; he turned his face away, but not before he had seen her lay her cheek briefly against the white container, then carefully set it down, next to the dust-laden boxes made of pine.

After she had fastened the door, she came to him and put her head on his shoulder. He felt her weariness flow into his bones and settle there, his burden now, and he closed his arms around her.

Later that evening, while she prepared their simple

supper, he sat at the oak table, which smelled of strong soap and gleamed with lemon oil. He felt brain-numbed, as though he had been the one anesthetized, unable to deal with the questions that tumbled about in his mind. Had he lost the child he would have given dreams to? Would another come along to test him—and would he then be ready?

But one calming revelation rested solid as a stone in his heart: he had, after all, reached a goal—had arrived, after making his way through choking vines of indecision, at a destination. Even if it turned out to be only a temporary stopping place on the way to something else, for now, he knew where he was. He was home.

*

# Shelter

Ellen emptied the contents of the sack onto the bed. "Emery boards, baby powder, knee-high stockings. And a shower cap, in the event that I can't talk them out of hosing you down." She talked mainly to surround herself with sound. The day before, she had uprooted and transplanted her mother as easily as if the woman were a small tree. Accomplished swiftly, the deed was as oppressive to Ellen as the stale air in this tiny room which was now her mother's only allotted space in the world.

Mrs. Quincy hovered over the objects with interest, like a hummingbird over a flower. "What is 'hosing me down'?" she asked.

"Mama, the rule here is that everyone has to take showers."

"I prefer baths. Tell them I want my bath every morning, just before breakfast. I missed my breakfast. No one brought it."

The words trickled out in a thin stream.

Ellen saw the chin quiver, the eyes mist with tears.

"Of course you did. Someone has combed your hair, helped you get dressed. I'm sure someone also brought you a breakfast tray."

"But I don't remember what I ate. Did I get my juice, prune and orange mixed together? I have to have that, first thing." Petulance was becoming panic.

"I put in that request yesterday. I watched the woman write it down on your chart."

At that moment, a nurse appeared in the doorway, briskly cheerful, her white uniform reassuringly crisp as paper. "All settled in, now, Annie? The night nurse said you slept like a baby."

"I wish to be called Mrs. Quincy." The quiver in her chin had moved to her voice.

Ellen explained. "She never has liked the name Annie. She really does prefer being called Mrs. Quincy, especially by people she doesn't know well."

The nurse frowned with the upper part of her face while the smile remained intact below. "We use first names here. Makes it more family like."

"What's your first name?" Mrs. Quincy asked politely.

"The rule doesn't necessarily apply to staff. I am Miss Darby, South Wing R.N., on duty from eight until four." Miss Darby whipped her arm into position, like the beginning of a salute, to read her watch. "Before I go, is there anything else you wish to tell me?" She had turned her back to the older woman and was speaking to Ellen.

Ellen said, also turning away from Mrs. Quincy, "I'd like for my mother to have sponge or tub baths, and in private."

Miss Darby frowned with her whole face. "The L.P.N. in charge of washing her is responsible for seven other residents. She wouldn't have time to sponge-bathe each one, and a private bath is out of the question in any event."

"But my mother objects to the indignity of a communal shower, as would I." She was paying, wasn't she? And the customer was always right?

Apparently not. "In the case of absolute necessity, such as patients who are bedridden or have casts, of course we make exception. But at this time there is no such reason why your mother can't take the shower. Which is only three times a week, by the way. Not every day."

"I'll discuss the matter with her doctor," Ellen said.

"The doctors cooperate with our rules." Miss Darby waved her hand toward the display of silver-framed photographs on the dresser. "You understand that the nursing home is not responsible for valuables. You've removed her jewelry, haven't you?"

"All but the wedding ring. I'm not going to take that from her."

Mrs. Quincy's eyes darted back and forth from the other women's faces as they talked. She placed her left hand, with the gold band on the third finger, behind her.

"Well, that's your risk. I do suggest you thumbtack the photographs on the bulletin board and take the frames home with you," Miss Darby said.

"If any of my mother's very few personal belongings disappear from this room, I'll question everyone here until I find the thief—" Ellen took a breath before she continued. "I don't mean to be belligerent. She's led a sheltered life, and all these rules are going to take some getting used to."

Miss Darby had moved to the doorway and was poised for flight. "But this is the ultimate sheltered life. The purpose of Sunset Haven is to provide a haven for those in their sunset years."

She was gone before Ellen could rejoin with, "And to turn a neat profit for those who own the place. . ."

Ellen smiled at her mother almost professionally, as though she herself were one of the staff. "I'm so glad your room has a view of the courtyard. Look, Mama. The forsythia is in bloom." She propelled the older woman to the window.

"That's not forsythia, that's jasmine. We used to have it all over the back fence. Your father would prune it himself, but it died the same year that he did. Just died out, and it's supposed to be a perennial. Did you sell the house?" Her eyes, behind the thick glasses, loomed large with an expression Ellen couldn't remember having seen before.

"Mama, you just left the house yesterday."

Mrs. Quincy clutched Ellen's arm. "You can't sell it, because it's in my name. I want to go home right now."

The unexpected asperity caused Ellen to respond sharply: "You can't live alone any longer. You nearly burned the place down."

"I certainly did not. What are you talking about?"

"See? You've forgotten already. You don't remember leaving the pot of soup boiling away on the stove all day long last week, do you? If that woman next door hadn't dropped by when she did, and that's another thing, your neighbors were tired of feeling they had to check on you —"

Mrs. Quincy interrupted. "Then take me to your house. Why can't I live with you?" She did not look at Ellen.

"Ah, Mama." Ellen put her arms around the thin shoulders. "It wouldn't work. David and the boys would get on your nerves. And you'd get on theirs."

"What boys?" Mrs. Quincy raised blank eyes.

"My sons. Your grandsons."

"Oh. I thought you meant my sons. My son—I just have one. His name is Scott."

"Mama, Scott died twenty-five years ago, in an automobile accident."

where periodically placed signs proclaimed in ominous black letters: FLOOR MAY BE SLIPPERY. Bernice led Mrs. Quincy into a large reception room. Glancing through the open doorway as she passed it, Ellen saw a young woman in a leotard explaining, in a loud, cheerful voice, to a line of old people in wheel chairs, how to raise their arms above their heads.

At three-thirty, slightly breathless from her fast walk from the parking lot at the rear of the building, Ellen entered Sunset Haven for the second time that day and was assaulted by the smell of disinfectant. Crepe paper streamers in bright colors were swathed skimpily across the entrance to the reception room; a few limp posters of elephants and lions were displayed on easels placed along the walls. Balloons were tied to the backs of wheelchairs. Their white heads drooping like flowers under a plethora of sunlight, the old people sat in a circle and dutifully clapped their hands to harsh calliope music from the record player.

Ellen's glance searched the group before she realized that her mother was sitting alone in the middle of the circle, wearing a conical hat with a cluster of cotton balls on the point. A purple ruff of accordion-folded paper encased Mrs. Quincy's neck like a surgical brace. Someone had painted bright red circles on her cheeks and the tip of her nose, and a huge, lipsticked grin exceeded the parameters of her prim, small mouth.

A uniformed attendant, not Bernice, sauntered

over. "You must be Annie's daughter. She's been asking for you."

"Why is my mother's face painted in this ridiculous fashion?" Ellen heard her voice rise, unsettled, pitching about like a rudderless boat in deep water.

"Why, she won the draw. Annie pulled the winning number from the magician's hat, so she got to be the clown! She's our special person of the day, aren't you, hon?" The woman patted Mrs. Quincy's shoulder and, gazing serenely ahead, moved past Ellen, who stood rooted in rage.

When she could move, Ellen knelt beside the chair, took her mother's hand, and pressed it to her own face.

From blackened rims, Mrs. Quincy's pale blue eyes brightened with recognition. Wreathed by the artificial grin, her voice was as lyrical and firm as birdsong: "Ellen, darling! I knew you would come to get me, as soon as you found out where I was."

Ellen could only watch as her mother's face took on a sudden radiance, a numinous glow that rose from the confines of the caricature to reflect—there was no doubt about it—a pure and genuine happiness.

# The Ritual

Harlan was waiting for certain things to happen that summer—his acne to clear up, his chin to firm up, his frame to lengthen. He was fourteen, and more than a little anxious to see some evidence of approaching manhood. He spent a lot of time observing people. He especially liked to watch the ten-year-old girl who had moved into the house next door, because he pitied and loathed her almost as much as he did himself, for the same reason: She was pathetic in her unfinished state.

Harlan's mother had volunteered him to mow the newcomers' yard. He had to make his own spending money because she was so tight—she wasn't ever going to let go of the Depression, even though it was 1940—and he didn't mind, much, cutting grass. The clanging noise of the lawn mower deafened the voices he sometimes heard; voices that put mischievous thoughts into his mind, such as, why didn't he steal money from his mother's sugar bowl and buy cigarettes with it. He had done that before, but for weeks afterward she mouthed about what had happened to a couple of lousy quarters. He was cutting their front yard for the first time when the girl came out with a book in her hand and plopped herself down in the porch swing. She lifted her face toward him timidly, but he pretended not to see, since she was so insignificant-looking with no bosom starting. He was glad he didn't have any little brat sisters or brothers.

"Hello," she called, just as the reel gave a squeaky sigh and stopped turning.

"Hello," he said, not pleasantly. The mower had slipped a gear; he should have greased the bearings. He squatted down and glared at the spiral blade, coated with rust and grass clippings.

"Is it broken?" she asked.

"I guess so," he said, and kicked it. He looked at her then; she was rapt with sympathy. "What's your name?"

"Laura," she said. "What's yours?"

"Harlan," he said. Not Jim, or Jake, or Tom: Harlan, which nobody could spell and which always elicited a sneer when someone heard it for the first time. The only guy he knew worse off was named Chauncey. He sighed and wiped his forehead with the back of his hand. "You got a Coke inside?"

She shook her head. "Just Kool-Aid. Wait here and I'll get you some." She had already started to open the screen door. She brought back half a Dixie cup full of pale green liquid without any ice. "My mother doesn't allow me to get out the ice trays. We have to save it for my dad." She was looking at him to see if he knew, and of course he did. Everyone knew her dad had TB.

"I heard he's sick," Harlan said, easing himself down on the top porch step. "Where is he?"

"He stays on a cot on the back porch. It's screened all around. He gets some sunshine that way without having to go outside, and it's cooler at night. We don't have an attic fan." She shrugged, embarrassed at confessing these failings.

"How come you all moved here when he was sick?" Harlan bit a hangnail off his thumb and allowed himself a moment of satisfaction; he'd been working at the thing off and on for a couple of days. He dreaded having to confront the lawn mower, lying inert as a sleeping dog where he'd left it. He really wasn't interested in his question at all. He didn't know why he had started such a dumb conversation.

"Because it's the only place we could come after he lost his job. That was my grandmother who lived here, and after she died—it was right after Christmas—the family was going to sell the house. But when Daddy got sick, they decided we could move in and stay here until he can work again." She smiled as though everything was all right.

Harlan frowned. "Yeah, I knew the place was empty

for a few months," he said. His own dad had a traveling job and was gone most of the time. (Harlan figured he probably had another woman in one of those little towns he went to on the edge of the state. He fantasized about it: She'd be attractive in a cheap-looking way, and lots younger than his mother.) But at least the old man brought in a paycheck and wasn't holed up in his pajamas on the back porch, coughing all day and using all the ice.

"Your mom works, doesn't she?" He yawned to show his lack of interest and started to uncoil himself from the steps.

"Just 'til three o'clock every day," Laura said. She was tagging along after him. "But I have to stay here with my dad until she gets home."

He dragged the resisting lawn mower behind him. "I got to get this fixed before I can finish the lawn. Tell your mom I'll get back to it soon's I can."

She was still following a few feet behind him when he got to the break in the hedge between their yards. Then he got the idea.

"What'd you say your name was—Laura?"

She nodded, pleased he'd remembered.

"Laura, I'm going to give you something to think about. That is, if you can keep a secret."

She hugged herself in anticipation. "Oh, I can."

He lowered his voice. "I happen to be a person who believes in ghosts. Do you?"

"I'm not sure." She shrugged. He exulted at the look on her face, which told him that she most certainly did believe in ghosts.

"It's possible, you know, to call up ghosts to places where they used to live, especially when the person has recently—gone on." He paused. She was hanging on his every word. Her eyes got bright as a cat's; her prim little mouth opened, rounded in suspense. Harlan spoke slowly in his new low voice. "Now, I would like to conduct an experiment that would require your secrecy as well as your participation."

She was actually holding her breath. If he didn't hurry and get to the point she might explode. But he enjoyed sounding like a teacher. She accorded him adult status; that must be why he was willing to stand out in the hot sun wasting his time talking to her. He cleared his throat to make his voice come out even deeper. "What I propose to do, Laura, is teach you a ritual that will call forth the ghost of your grand-mother." He folded his arms and waited for her to finish absorbing what he'd said.

She had backed away a few steps so that she was well within the boundaries of her own yard. For a second he thought she would turn and run and he would have lost her forever. But she sighed, and brushed her bangs from her forehead with both hands. Finally she stopped twitching and fiddling with her hair—he wouldn't have been surprised if she started to suck on her thumb—and she said, "Okay. I guess so. Is it hard? I mean, are you sure I can learn to do it?"

"Absolutely. We'll start tomorrow. Don't tell a soul though. Secrecy is imperative. Understand?" Harlan would have dismissed her then anyway, even if he hadn't seen his mother appear on his own front porch. He had already begun to devise the ritual, letting the details fall in place in his mind, in a surge of omnipotence that obliterated all concern about his pimples, his scrawniness, and his disgust with the way life was treating him in general.

His mother's exasperated comments, as she took in the situation— broken lawn mower, job unfinished— pelted him like stinging rain. "When are you going to learn to keep that thing in good order? Did she pay you anything at all? Looks like you got almost half the front cut anyway." He whistled his way past her.

"Har-lan!" She yelled as he went inside, slamming the screened door practically in her face. He didn't blame his dad one bit for staying out of town as much as possible. "Harlan," she repeated, following him up the stairs, "did you go inside that house?"

"I just went to the edge of the porch. I was sorry for the kid, she's left there alone to look out for her dad. She offered me something to drink, and I took it, because it was hot as hell."

His mother let the "hell" go by, she was so anxious to get to the main point. "Oh, my heavens, Harlan, you didn't drink out of one of their glasses, did you? That's how TB germs are spread!"

"It was a paper cup," Harlan said. He remembered he had tossed the wadded cup into the shrubbery; he felt kind of bad about that. Maybe tomorrow he'd retrieve it and put it in a garbage can. Tomorrow, when he figured out how he could teach the kid his "ritual" without his mother knowing he was over there getting contaminated.

Laura's mother backed her old green Chevy out of the driveway at 8:15, and his mother left just a few minutes later in their old blue Ford to do marketing. She'd make that last all morning. Harlan was ringing the doorbell at exactly 8:30. When Laura answered, he got right to the point. "I'm ready to teach you the ritual."

She put a finger to her lips. "Shhh," she said. "Daddy expects me to stay in the house where he can call out to me."

"He's not that helpless, is he?" Harlan hadn't considered the daddy to be a hindrance.

"He just likes to know where I am," she said.

"Oh, well, it was just an idea. Forget it," Harlan said, starting to move away from the door. Dumb kid.

"No, I really want to learn it," Laura said. "Wait for me out by our hammock. He can't see us there but I can run back and check on him quick enough."

Harlan had to admit that it was a well-chosen

setting. The hammock swung between two oak trees in the side yard. The shady spot wasn't highly visible from either house or the street.

"What did you tell him?" He asked when she came out a few minutes later. He was waiting beside the hammock, feeling a little foolish. He'd been keener on the idea the day before.

"I told him I was going outside to read so I could get some fresh air," she said. "He knows children need fresh air, and he doesn't really want me to stay out on the porch with him because of—well, he just doesn't."

"Are you sure you want to do this?" he asked. The atmosphere didn't seem spooky enough; he'd never convince her in the daylight.

"I'm sure," she said eagerly. "I always liked my grandmother. She'd be a good ghost. And I want to ask her questions."

"You didn't tell your mom anything about it, did you?"

"Of course I didn't! You told me not to." She turned her face toward him with such a trusting look that Harlan almost told her the truth: that he didn't know one damn thing about calling up ghosts. She held out a neatly folded man's handkerchief and said, "I figured you'd have to blindfold me, so you can use this."

He opened his mouth wide in mock surprise. "I certainly do have to blindfold you, but how'd you know?"

"I just did. And I'll tell you something else." She flashed a bold smile at him. "I know my grandmother's going to come. I've been having dreams that she would. That's why you were sent to teach me the ritual, isn't it?"

Harlan wished with all his heart that Jake, his almost friend, Jake who sometimes fooled around with him when he didn't have better things to do, could be here to hear this crazy kid! He could hear himself telling Jake, mimicking her thin little pip-squeak voice: "That's why you were sent to teach me the ritual, isn't it?" And then: "Jake, I'm thinking, what ritual? I'm just standing there wondering how the hell I ever got started with such a stupid joke in the first place, and this kid gets totally dead serious about contacting her dead grandmother in the spook world. So, what did I do? Well, I gave her a ritual, all right! I made up a whole string of stuff—"

Jake would shake his head admiringly. What a joker Harlan was! The word would get out . . .

"Here we go," Harlan said, rubbing his hands together. "First we tie the blindfold. Not too tight. That okay?" He adjusted the fold of cloth across her nose and tied it behind her head. She nodded. "And now, Laura, you must do as I say. Get in the hammock. That's right, lie back. First, you will count from one hundred backward. When you get to one, say your grandmother's full name three times, very slowly." He paused. She was straining with tense concentration. "Got that?" he said sternly. She bobbed her head up and down like a chicken. "After the third time, you can begin to talk to her, just as though she's here. And when you get the feeling that she's really present, sort of indicate to me so I'll know." He sat down on the ground. Might as well not be above the level of the hedge, just in case someone looked over there. Maybe the blindfold wasn't a good idea.

"Do I count out loud?"

"Sure," Harlan said. "Not too loud, though. And when you want to end the session, just say good-bye, and begin to count forward to a hundred."

They went through the procedure three times. After each time, she looked at him questioningly. He was beginning to be bored to death, especially with all the counting. Finally, she sat up and pulled the blindfold off. "I can't seem to make contact," she said.

Make contact! Harlan almost swooned. "Well, I think you need to practice it by yourself," he said. "I'm an outsider, after all. Your grandmother didn't know me. I mean, I never exchanged two words with her. So it figures that even though I am the chosen method by which you will make contact, that contact will be a private affair between you and her." He was proud of it. He always could talk himself out of situations; he had a talent for it, his mom said.

"How soon should I try again?" Laura asked. Her

face was flushed from effort and from the blindfold. She looked like a bird that had hatched too soon. Harlan turned away in disgust.

"You must practice it at least ten times a day," he said, relishing the cruelty. "Whenever you can get away from your dad or whatever. But you should always come to the hammock; the ritual won't work anywhere else."

"You think it'd be better if I came at night?" She implored him with her eyes to say no.

"Sure, it'd be a whole lot better if you slipped out here and did it at night," Harlan said. "Just don't get caught."

"I'm a little bit scared of the dark." She bit her lip. "Couldn't you—"

"Oh, all right," he said. "I'll come out tonight and keep you company the first time. But you have to learn not to be afraid of the dark. Ghosts love the dark."

"What time?" She said. "What time will you be here?"

"After supper. Eight. Can you really slip out without your folks knowing?" Could he, for that matter? "Harlan, where are you going?" his mother would call at the very first creak of the stairs if she heard him coming down—he always holed up in his room listening to the radio after supper.

"Mama sits on the back porch with Daddy after she does the dishes. She doesn't even know when I go to bed. She won't think I'm anywhere but in my room."

She stiffened. "I think I heard him calling. I'd better go see what he wants. I'll see you tonight."

Harlan watched her run zigzaggedly, like a rabbit, down the side of the yard and toward the back of her house. He felt conspicuous standing out there by himself. When he got back to his house, his mom was just driving into the driveway; she hadn't seen him over there, he was sure.

She sent him out to clip the hedge across the back of their own yard after lunch and he saw, out of the side of his eye, Laura's skinny figure gliding into the hammock. She was tying the blindfold on herself. Then she was lying there, the hammock motionless; undoubtedly, she was putting herself through the "ritual." Stupid girl. It had been so easy convincing her it almost wasn't any fun.

His dad came in unexpectedly from a road trip, which meant Harlan only got one piece of chicken for supper. "Come on, son," his dad said, as soon as the meal was over. "Might as well get on to that broken lawn mower or we'll never hear the last of it." He rolled his eyes toward Harlan's mom.

So the two of them went out to the garage and Harlan's dad worked on the lawn mower and made wisecracks, mostly about Harlan's mom. Harlan enjoyed it. They were just shooting the breeze about lots of things when all of a sudden his dad said, "Hey, you should come with me on the road tomorrow. I'll be going near that fishing camp I told you about; we might even get through my calls in time to fish for a coupla hours."

Harlan said he might as well, since all he had to do was everybody on the block's yard work, and it would just get put off longer. They laughed. It was after eight when his dad wiped the grease off his hands and said, "Okay, that does it. Try not to be clumsy and break it again, buddy," and they started back across the darkened yard to the house. Harlan saw the hammock through a gap in the hedge. Silly Laura was just standing there beside it, probably scared out of her wits. She looked like a little ghost herself in the moonlight.

Well, he couldn't go over there with his dad home. He thought of calling her on the telephone later and explaining that he'd be gone for a few days —his dad said they would spend at least one night on the road— and she'd just have to forget it til he got back. But, what if her mother answered?

Before he went to bed, he looked out his upstairs window and across the hedge, dark as pitch even in the moonlight, and he could see the hammock swinging back and forth by itself; Laura must have just left, but she was nowhere in sight. It was ten o'clock—had she spent two whole hours out there in the dark waiting for him? He felt goose pimples start skipping about on his arms. Maybe she had been out there all that time trying to conjure up a ghost by herself! The thing could get out of hand, she could get too frightened or something and tell someone what he'd told her! Finally, Harlan punched his pillow into the shape he liked best, closed his eyes for sleep, and willed himself to forget about the whole thing; he had a little vacation, traveling with his dad, to look forward to.

As it turned out, he really didn't give the subject more than an occasional thought the whole time— three days—they were gone. They got home on a Friday afternoon, and Harlan felt like he'd been gone a month. His mom hugged him like he had. He was sunburned from the fishing and she said she thought it had helped his acne. He wished she hadn't mentioned the pimples in front of his dad, who had never seemed to notice the problem, but at least she had given him a compliment.

"What did you two talk about all that time by yourselves?" his mom asked them. Harlan tried to remember. He had wanted to ask his dad all kinds of things but he hadn't. He waited for his dad to answer her, but he ignored the question, too.

"So what's been going on here in the boondocks?" His dad always said that to her when he'd been gone.

"That poor man next door died the day after you all left, and the funeral was yesterday. I took a cake over there and it's really sad, just that woman and the little girl. I expect they'll be moving soon back to where her people are, somewhere in Georgia. I do wish you'd finish cutting their lawn now, Harlan. And I don't think you should charge."

He went over the next morning when he saw Laura come out on the porch. She seemed to be expecting him.

"Sorry about your dad," he said. "I had to go out of town with my dad, and I couldn't get word to you to say why I didn't come back that night to go through—well, anyway. I'm sorry about that, too. Mom said I should finish your lawn today." He dared to look at her then, but she didn't appear to be too sad. He had thought she'd be pink-eyed from crying. He had never realized her dad was all that sick.

"I did just like you told me to," she said, shyly. "I went through it about ten times that first day, and I tried again for a long time that night by myself. Nothing happened. Then, the next day, after the doctor came and said Daddy was dying—I mean, Mama and I already knew, because he had been rattling so, much worse than ever before—well, I went back to the hammock and went through the ritual and that's when she came through."

He couldn't believe what he was hearing. "Came through?" The words, his echo of hers, hung there between them stark as chalk on a blackboard. She was onto him and it was going to be her time to joke. He said, almost pleadingly, "You're kidding, aren't you?" The whirring noise of crickets and June bugs had suddenly intensified. Blackbirds were carrying on, chattering like they knew something.

"I wouldn't kid about it," Laura said, frowning. "She came through so clear I could see her good as I can that nightgown on your mother's clothesline."

Harlan looked over to where his mother's night-gown was flopping around weirdly in a gust of wind.

"Oh, that's all you saw," he said. "She's always got those old things hanging out there. She must have a million of them."

"No, it's not." She looked at him as though she felt sorry for him. "I really saw my grandmother. She was standing about twenty feet from me; she was just like I remember her, in the dress she had on when she had that picture made that hangs on the wall in our living room. Would you like to see it?"

"No," Harlan said truthfully. He didn't want to see an old picture of a dead person he'd never even known. He couldn't remember ever having seen her grand-mother over once or twice when she was alive. She must have looked like any other old woman. He wouldn't remember; no image came to him. But the enormity of what Laura had said was sinking like a weight in his stomach. It was a lie that she didn't know she was telling.

He wanted to leave, to go jump on his bike and ride off somewhere, but he knew he had to put a stop to whatever it was he'd started. He said, "Look, I might as well just tell you straight out. I played a joke on you. I mean, I just wanted to kid around a little for something to do. I didn't expect you to really go at it like that. Well, maybe I did expect you to, but only for a while. I thought you'd see I was making the whole thing up." He could hardly watch her face.

She sighed, a grown-up sigh. "I'm glad you taught me the ritual. We don't have to move for awhile—not until the house is sold anyway —and I'm going to keep doing it because I think my grandmother will bring Daddy back to see me, too. In fact," she said, flushed with pleasure and triumph, "She even said she would!"

With that the blackbirds chorused anew. Oh hell, Harlan thought. "She talks too?" he whispered.

"She's just started to. But I don't know whether she will talk around you, or not. What do you think?"

"I told you what I think. I think you took something seriously that was meant to be a damn fool joke." He welcomed the anger that had begun to replace fear. His voice steadied. "And you'd better stop imagining all these things or you'll end up in the loony bin. You really will, so stop right now, you hear?" He was practically shouting.

Laura's mother came out of the house and looked toward him. "Oh, you're going to finish the yard. Good," she said, and turned to go back inside.

Wait, he wanted to yell. Wait, lady, you got a crazy-talking girl out here, better come get her and lock her up inside the house, away from that hammock!

Laura smiled like she knew what he was thinking. "I don't need you to be involved in it, anyway. You don't have to feel bad about showing me. I'm glad you did, I really am!"

"For the hundredth time, I'm telling you, I made it all up, out of thin air! It can't work, it's not a ritual, it's not anything! It was just a joke!" Harlan kicked the lawn mower. He wanted to shake her.

"I know you think you made it up," she said softly. "But it's a real ritual, and it must have been all along, because it works." She turned and went inside her house, not looking back at him.

Harlan thought about Laura and her unbudgable stupidity a lot during the next few days, but he couldn't think what more he could do about the mess he had started, so finally he decided to consider the matter closed. He didn't hang around home any more than necessary; he made himself ride his bike for long periods of time in other neighborhoods. And he tried not to look over toward the hammock, even in the daytime, but he could close his eyes and see Laura swinging in the thing, pushing it off with one foot, one arm thrown across her eyes.

Finally, what he dreaded happened; her mother called and asked him to mow their lawn again. The grass had gotten pretty high; it would take twice as long to cut it. He told his mom so, but she made him go anyway. He whistled while he pushed the mower and didn't look in the direction of the house at all. But when he was through, he knew he had to go up the steps to the porch and ring the doorbell. Laura came to the door. Behind her, shadowy in mid-morning darkness— the window shades were pulled down to keep out the heat— was the living room where he'd never been, where the picture of her grandmother was.

"Come on in, Harlan," Laura said. She sounded normal. "We have lemonade if you want some."

He wanted to go in, but his feet wouldn't move forward. He wasn't afraid of TB germs, he knew that. He just couldn't go inside that creepy house where everybody died. He shook his head. "No thanks," he said. His own voice came out pretty normal too, so he relaxed a little. "You still doing that crazy stuff?" He was surprised to hear himself ask the question.

"It's not crazy," she said serenely. "I've made contact with Daddy, too."

Harlan felt his skin lift all over his body like it was going to fly off him. He laughed as loud as he could make himself in order to obliterate the sound of her words with a sound of his own. He turned and crossed the long width of the porch—it seemed like a mile—to the steps. He hardly felt his feet make contact. He grabbed the handle of the lawn mower with relief and held onto it tightly, as though doing so would keep him in touch with the earth, and he was through the opening in the hedge before he felt himself breathe again. He hadn't said another word to her. He didn't care whether she thought he was acting weird or not, because he knew now for a fact that she was absolutely crazy. By the time he got safely inside his own house, its familiar shabbiness as reassuring as a hug, he was secure in the knowledge that he was no longer involved whatsoever in whatever was going on in that girl's head.

Toward the end of the summer, just before school was due to start, Laura and her mother moved away. Harlan's dad had found him a part-time job doing clean-up work for a store downtown, so he hadn't had to mow the neighborhood lawns anymore. He heard about the move from his mom, who had tried to be friendly to Laura's mother since the tragedy, but from a distance, across the hedge. He was relieved when she told him.

The day the moving van came, Harlan went over and took the hammock down from the hooks on the trees and folded it neatly and handed it to one of the movers. He wondered why he had been somewhat scared before, being at her house that last time. He could view the whole thing now with detachment. Of course, Laura would outgrow the nonsense; believing all that stuff was just a way to get herself through a bad time. But maybe she'd like to have the old hammock, maybe someday she could even laugh about what she'd used it for. Anyway, he didn't want it to be forgotten. If there were any spooks, they were hers, and he didn't want them coming back to an abandoned hammock in the yard next door. Laura didn't appear while he was there. After that he watched from his upstairs window until the van was loaded, the doors slammed shut. Then he watched Laura and her mother put the last boxes and a couple of suitcases in their car.

Harlan ran from his room, down the stairs, out the front door. The van was just pulling out into the street and Laura's mother was revving up her motor to follow. Harlan practically threw himself at the car. "Wait!" he yelled, and the woman slammed on brakes, turned a startled face toward him. "I have to say something," he explained. They looked at him, Laura with as much blank curiosity as her mom.

"I just want to say that I put the hammock in the van for you. I mean, it looked like you had forgotten it."

Laura leaned toward the open window. "I was leaving it for you," she said. "I hoped you would use it so you'd find out for yourself that the ritual really works."

Laura's mother said, "What on earth—?" but she was watching the van, already halfway down the block. "We have to go. Please get back from the car, Harlan."

Harlan ran alongside on the sidewalk as the car began to move. He stopped as it picked up speed. Laura was still looking back at him through the window as the car rounded the corner; her face paled in the distance, like a mysterious moon, disappearing from view.

# Penolia

The first time she used the power, Penolia placed her hands firmly on the shoulder of a woman who was complaining about her bursitis and said, as though she knew what she was talking about, "The laying on of hands can cure just about anything." She closed her eyes and willed it. When the woman declared that the pain really had left at Penolia's touch, a couple of bystanders showed some interest, but Frank crumpled his empty beer can in one hand, showing off his own power, grabbed Penolia by the elbow, and steered her out the door. "You better not try none of that witching on me," he said.

From the moment she'd met Frank a few weeks before in the restaurant where she was a waitress, Penolia had wanted only to please him. She had been with him ever since, except when she was at work. She was eighteen, and had never loved a man before Frank. He now had more of her than she had of herself.

When they were in bed that night Frank said, in his teasing voice, "Think you could cure yourself of a broken arm if I was to give you one?"

"I don't know," Penolia replied truthfully. Could she cure herself of a broken heart when the time came? She looked at him in the moonlight that seeped through the window screen and hung like something solid over the lumpy mattress where they lay. He was handsomer than anybody on television. She closed her eyes, holding in the private space behind her eyelids the gleam of his thick black hair, the sheen of his golden skin. Her own skin was white and freckled. He had told her he didn't like freckles, but would overlook them in her case. She decided that the baby would have his looks.

But Frank was gone before the baby came. When it was close to her time, she left the town to go home, over the mountain. She got off the bus at her daddy's private road that cut through a waist-high thicket of Queen Anne's lace. The sight of those wild flowers (that looked like doilies her mama had crocheted to put around on the furniture) brought tears to her eyes. She hadn't known how homesick she was.

Her daddy saw her first and clumped across the field to meet her. When he took in her condition his face swirled like a calm river surprised by a storm. "Where's your husband, girl?" He looked past her, hoping to see someone else coming up the road.

"No husband, Daddy."

He made his face get back into shape, then took her suitcase; at least he could relieve her of that burden. "Tell me who he is," he said, his voice like low thunder.

"He wasn't from anywhere around here. Now he's probably in Texas. That's where he said he was going."

"How come he didn't take you with him?"

"He was scared of me," she said, not wanting to admit that Frank had never loved her, not in the least. "Because I possess a power."

"A power, huh? But not the kind to make him do right by you," her daddy said sourly. Then: "What kind of power?"

"It just came to me a while back. I used it to cure a woman's shoulder pain. Next I fixed a man's back after he threw it out and was like to being paralyzed. I got a colicky baby quiet after it had cried solid for three days." She could have told him more, but the look on his face stopped her.

"Sounds like something that comes from the devil," her daddy said. They had come to the hard, swept ground up close to the house. "And if it is, girl, I don't want your mama to know about it. She's a good Christian woman who doesn't deserve a daughter who's taken to witching."

Penolia flinched, but all she said was, "Seems to me if the power helps people, it would have to come from God, wouldn't it?"

"Not necessarily. That old devil speaks with silken

tongue," her daddy said.

"Forked tongue," Penolia corrected.

"You know a lot about him, seems like."

When she saw Penolia, her mama came down the front porch steps like someone was chasing her. "Oh, my stars above," she said.

"I thought he would marry me, Mama." It was the best she could offer, even if it wasn't but half true. "I'll leave with my baby soon's I can. We won't be trouble to you for long, I promise." But her mama had wrapped her in a strong hug that felt better than anything since the last time Frank made love to her, before the morning she woke to find a note on the dresser that said, "So long, sugar, if I could spell your name I'd write it here. By the way, be sure to name the kid for me. Frank Jr. or Frances, you could call her Frankie."

That morning, as Penolia left Frank's boarding house for the last time, she turned and looked up at the window of the drab room where they'd locked together and made the baby. In place of the crackled orange paper roller-shades, crisp white curtains waved like flags. The longer she stared at the house, the better it looked. The blistering paint smoothed out; the porch no longer sagged. She hoped that would make up for the fact that Frank had left owing considerable rent—she'd paid some, but not all, of it.

At the restaurant, after collecting her wages with which she would buy the bus ticket, she tried to will the grease-coated kitchen clean, but suddenly she knew it wouldn't work. She'd used all the available energy for that day on the landlady's house.

Penolia knew her folks would react just as they did about her condition; first they'd be upset, then they would accept. But they insisted on having her power checked out by the preacher, who asked her first thing, "Do you invoke the name of Jesus Christ when you call on this power?"

"No sir. I just touch the place that has the problem, or think about it hard. It doesn't take but a few seconds if the place is on a person."

"You mean you use it in other ways?"

Penolia decided not to tell him about touching up the landlady's house. "I think it's intended mainly for healing physical pain," she amended.

"Hmm. You may be in cahoots with Satan."

"Oh, no, I don't call on him, either."

"If you don't specify which power, good or evil, the devil chooses for you. You're doing his bidding." The preacher wiped his face with his handkerchief and looked as spent as if he'd just delivered the Sunday sermon.

"I don't believe that's true, sir," Penolia protested.

"My girl may have got herself in trouble, but there isn't anything evil about her," her mama spoke up then. "If God saw fit to put a special power in her hands, then He knows she'll see fit to use it wisely." The preacher didn't have a comeback for that reasoning.

The baby, a girl, was born with hair dark as the mountain at night and skin the pale amber of honeysuckle—made, as Penolia had visualized, in Frank's image—but Penolia didn't name her Frances and call her Frankie. She named her Queen Anne and most of the time called her Little Queen. Penolia's folks took to the baby and didn't want them to leave right away. Little Queen would be better off spending her babyhood in the fresh mountain air, surrounded by family love.

Penolia was called on by the people of neighboring farms before they even tried the old remedies of roots and herbs and cider vinegar, and most of the time, her will was enough to banish their ills. She didn't ask for payment, but accepted whatever was offered: coins, fresh-caught fish, a whittled toy for the child, smoke-cured bacon. She was much admired for her gift, but the preacher didn't invite her to do laying on of hands in the church.

She had known, somewhere in the back of her mind, that the day would come when her power would be put to the test. She also knew it would concern Little Queen, who, at two years old, was as beautiful as an angel. The day it happened, Penolia had gone to the town in her daddy's truck. Holding Little Queen's hand, she came out of the hardware store and saw Frank across the street, standing beside his beat-up old red

Camaro (which now had a Texas license plate). She gathered Little Queen in her arms, climbed into the pickup and tried to hunch over sideways so Frank wouldn't recognize her if he looked that way. "Put your head in my lap and go to sleep," she said, and the child did so. She eased the truck out into the street, but he had seen her. She drove as fast as she dared with him in pursuit, honking his horn. The red dust rose like a protective curtain behind her after she hit the unpaved mountain road, but still he followed.

When she stopped near the house, he pulled up beside her. She looked at his face then. His hair was dull as a dusty crow's wing (and she had thought it gleaming), his cheeks were sallow and sunken. He wasn't nearly as handsome as she remembered him. "Hey, little mama," he said lazily as he got out of the car and stretched. "I came to see my baby boy."

"You don't have a claim to any baby here." She kept her hand on Little Queen's head in her lap.

"I dreamed it clear as life," he said. "I had me a little son in Georgia with hair black as mine, skin color of mine, face like mine." He came toward the truck.

Little Queen opened her eyes. Suddenly, Penolia knew what she had to will. The power surged behind her brain; the leaves on the trees trembled with the force of her concentration; bluejays and sparrows ceased their chatter and swooped up into the trees to hide.

Frank saw the child as she raised herself to a sitting

position on the front seat of the truck. The curiosity on his face gave way to astonishment. Penolia also marveled at what she had wrought: Little Queen's hair was whiter than field corn and her skin was dotted with pumpkin-colored freckles, some near the size of a dime. The ears that had lain flat against her head stuck out like Penolia's daddy's. Her nose now curved into a point, a trait often found in Penolia's mama's people; her eyes were slanted and yellow-green as scuppernongs. (Some of Penolia's kin, whose parents had been first cousins, had eyes like that.)

Frank let out a sigh of dismay. "A girl, and she ain't even pretty." Little Queen didn't seem to know he was talking about her. She looked happy and self-confident as always. Frank shifted his gaze from the child's face to the ground as he said, "I was gonna take both of you back to Texas with me." But even as he spoke the words, Penolia knew that idea was a thing of the past; Frank was back in his car, revving up the motor.

"No, thank you, we don't wish to go," she said anyway.

He leaned out the car window to look at the child again, and said, his voice sad, "I really didn't care whether it was a boy or a girl. I just knew, somehow, that the kid would have my stamp. I drove clear across the country thinking that I had myself a look-alike here. Well, she must take after your people, cause she sure as hell don't favor none of mine."

He hadn't even asked what the child's name was.

By the time Penolia's daddy came in from the back field and her mama from the church women's meeting, Little Queen's hair had darkened as easily as day changing to night; the freckles were gone, and her features were back to normal. Penolia saw no reason to tell anyone about Frank's visit.

For the next few weeks, Penolia was in a bad humor. Her folks didn't ask what was wrong. They were more embarrassed by the fact that Penolia had the power than they were by the fact that her baby had no father. When a neighbor came by and wanted a quick cure for his sprained ankle, Penolia snapped at him and told him he'd just have to let nature take its course. She said she wasn't God and shouldn't be expected to fix everything.

But the power still lay upon her like a gossamer cloak. She could look out on her daddy's farmland and if her gaze intensified in a certain way, the corn got taller and thicker. Sometimes she looked up the road that disappeared over the curve of the mountain, not toward the town, but in the direction of cities and a whole world where she'd never been. Although she tried not to acknowledge what had been taking shape in the back of her mind, Penolia found herself willing it anyway. She wasn't surprised when a motorcycle bounced up her daddy's private road at a hard fast clip late one afternoon. Even before she saw the stranger's face, she knew that she and Little Queen would leave with him. It didn't matter what he looked like, because she would never love someone for his looks again, anyway.

She gathered a bundle of their belongings, left a scrawled note on the kitchen table ("We're gone— Love always, Penolia") and was back on the porch before the bike came to a stop, scattering a fine spray of rocks. He said her name like he was tasting fresh peach ice cream for the first time: "Penolia."

If the power wasn't from God, then, according to the preacher, it had to be from—but Penolia smiled trustingly at the stranger as she and Little Queen climbed on behind him. As they left, the roar of the bike blended into a sudden clap of thunder; in fact, as some would recall later, the day ended with a rainbow storm, the kind where the sun shines even though it's raining, which means the devil is taking himself a wife. Her folks chose to believe that the rascal who abandoned Penolia before the baby was born had a change of heart and came to get them. Who else could have lured Penolia away?

# Conversation

There had been no hospital vigil, no hushed conferences with doctors, no watching life ebb away through tubes. One minute Michael was drying himself with a large, monogrammed, maroon towel after his shower and the next minute he was dead, slumped to the floor in a semi-sitting position, his arms dangling over the bathtub.

He had taken very good care of himself: stopped smoking years before, worked out at the athletic club three times a week. Still in his early fifties, he had already begun to delegate the more stressful work to younger partners and associates in the law firm. Although his internist and close friend Tom Jarrell had never detected any sign of a heart or vascular problem, Michael had kept up with the latest medical procedures in restorative surgery, just in case.

"You said that by the time you needed it, a quadruple bypass would be a piece of cake." Alone with her late afternoon drink in the tiny enclosed courtyard garden, Martha spoke aloud. She had begun to talk to him, as though he could hear her, soon after the funeral—actually, the day after Carol, their only child, had left.

"Daddy planned everything so you'll have no money worries. He always did think of us first, didn't he?" Carol's eyes had misted with fresh tears as she gave her mother a final hug before striding away toward her plane.

A fledgling attorney who was "going for it" (as her father had encouraged her to) with a huge law firm in another state, Carol had spent a week helping Martha with the transition from wife to widow. Martha was both resentful of and almost pathetically grateful for her daughter's efficiency; of course Carol was devastated over her father's death—but she wasn't immobilized by it.

"I know she doesn't mean to, but she makes me feel inadequate." Those were her first words to Michael, spoken after she got back from taking Carol to the airport. She heard the sound of her own voice as if it were a guest's. The dark green leaves on the potted gardenia bush quivered as though she were speaking to them. She almost thought of his death as a suicide because he had succumbed without resistance, as he might have yielded to an inevitable legal conclusion. "Did you think I wasn't capable of taking care of you through a long illness?" Of course she didn't really expect an answer from his essence, which permeated the house like remnants of cigarette smoke after a party.

Carol had gone though her father's papers—the family history he'd been writing, his carefully labeled files—before she packed everything in boxes with new labels. Next, she gave his clothes to the Salvation Army. Michael's three-button vested suits and wingtip shoes would be worn by derelicts. When Martha protested, Carol said, "Mother, he would want his clothes to go to people who can use them. Besides, it would be too depressing to keep these things that remind you of him around."

But everything reminded her of him. The dulled arms of his leather chair, the bottle of Scotch that was kept in the kitchen cabinet beside the corn flakes—she mixed her own afternoon drinks now, not bothering with the pewter jigger he had always measured with— even that reminded her of him. She put it in the drawer with screwdrivers and other things she never used. "I know exactly how much whiskey an ounce and a half is. I know where it comes to in the glass without having to measure," she said.

On the other side of the seven-foot pink brick wall was someone else's courtyard. The residents of the townhouse complex they'd moved into the year before were all middle-aged or older couples whose children were grown and gone, who respected each other's privacy. She never heard more than a muffled murmur or a delicate laugh, like a thin glass breaking, from beyond the wall. It wouldn't do for someone to hear her talking to Michael when he'd been dead for almost a month, so she tried to remember to keep her voice just above a whisper, as she used to when they talked in bed at night before and after making love, to prolong the intimacy.

"You won't see the grandchildren, if there ever are any," she said sadly, and a trifle smugly. She would be the favored grandparent by default. She wouldn't take a back seat to a handsome, silver-haired grandfather. She changed the subject. "Carol wants to book me on a museum tour to London next month. She has suggested that I get into another afternoon bridge foursome and enroll in continuing education courses. She says I myself am capable of teaching flower arranging, and that I should advertise for students. Her intention is that my days be filled completely. She doesn't realize that I've had my fill of filled days." She turned her head, feeling a gaze upon her. The peppercorn-sized eyes belonged to a rusty-flanked, gray-breasted bird, perched like an ornament in a limb of the dwarf cherry tree, which was the only thing besides miniature ivy that was planted around the patio.

"Go away," she said sternly. The bird cocked its tufted head and protested in a staccato of whistled syllables. Martha drained the last of her drink and went inside to put a carton of frozen lasagna in the microwave oven. Like most of their friends, she and Michael had been on a cholesterol-lowering diet for months. She had bought special mayonnaise and margarine, made muffins from oat bran, and concocted meatless main dishes. The frozen diet casseroles Carol bought for her were tastier and simpler.

The telephone rang eerily. She always thought Michael's disembodied voice was going to be on the other end; that's how they first communicated from the other side, she'd once read. "Hello," she said, holding her breath.

"Just checking in. You okay?" Carol sounded like a young child again. As though she needed her mother's reassurance.

"I'm fine," Martha said. Truthfully. She was absolutely all right.

The next time the phone rang, it was Tom Jarrell's wife Ann, inviting her to go to dinner with them.

"Thanks, but I've just had mine," Martha said. Remains of the pasta had already been scraped into the sink and whirred through the disposal.

Ann said, guilt lacing her voice as though it were somehow her fault that she still had a husband and Martha didn't, "I know it's hard to get through the cocktail hour by yourself."

No, it's not. Aloud, Martha said, "Actually, I'm limiting myself to one drink per session. Michael used to tell me that was a good habit to get into when you're by yourself."

The other woman laughed with embarrassment, as if Martha had shared some bedroom secret with her.

The next day the same bird was on a windowsill when Martha opened the bedroom curtains. Whenever she looked out, off and on, he was in evidence. She did not go out into the rectangle of captured sunset, which intensified the pinkness of the brick, to have her drink that afternoon. She surrounded herself with sounds of Schumann on the compact disc player. At least she had figured out how to work that without having to ask Carol to show her. She had brought her dinner on a tray into the sunroom when she glimpsed the bird on the outside of the floor-to-ceiling glass wall, clinging with flimsy legs to the narrow, almost ground-level ledge, staring at her with his round eyes. She tapped with her foot on the glass to scare him away, but he responded with a flirtatious flap of wings. She closed the blinds, irritated that she had to shut out the fixed, serene view and the last of the day's light.

The bird was back on the sill of the bedroom window the following morning, amid fresh milky-gray droppings on dried dung from the day before. After her breakfast Martha armed herself with the kitchen broom and went out, but the bird, chirping incomprehensibly, was in the tree, beyond her reach. Silent and resolute, she gripped the broom handle in both hands. As soon as the bird swooped down in a graceful (perhaps even trusting) arc, she thrashed wildly until the wedge of stiff bristles made contact with the small body, knocking it to the ground like a shuttlecock. She felt her own heart beating as frantically as the bird's must have been, but she could not bring herself to look closely, so she didn't know if she had actually knocked the floppy thing senseless. She spent the rest of the day shopping and at a movie matinee.

During her call that night, Carol said, "I think you should get a dog to keep you company. I seem to remember a cocker spaniel when I was very small. Wouldn't you like another one?"

Martha remembered that the spaniel had never been housebroken, had largely been ignored by all of them, had finally run away or been stolen, and hadn't been replaced. She said, "Darling, believe me: I do not want a dog, and I do not want a bird."

"Well, I certainly wasn't going to suggest a parakeet," Carol said.

When the cleaning woman arrived the next morning, Martha asked her to look around the courtyard for a wounded bird. "I saw it fall there yesterday," she explained, adding apologetically, "I'm squeamish about things like that myself." She watched from the doorway as the other woman bent over to poke about the ivy bed.

"Nothing there," the woman said, straightening up and looking at her with suspicion. The bird didn't appear that day or the next. On the third day, as Martha was about to leave to have her hair done, she saw a cat sitting sphinx-like on the courtyard wall. A sleek Siamese, the color of her mink coat and quite obviously male, it was wearing a leather collar. The animal was still there when she returned two hours later, so she called the neighbors, but no one had any idea whose it was.

The cat moved quietly and noiselessly about the courtyard all afternoon. When Martha took her Scotch-and-water outside, she addressed it directly: "I don't know much about cats, except that I've heard they're clean and are born housebroken. Is that so?"

The cat yawned and licked its paws and ignored her.

The next day she bought cat food, the most expensive brand in the store, and still it smelled revolting when she opened the can. She put the dish on the patio near the cherry tree. The cat appeared on top of the wall suddenly and solidly, as if materializing from a dream, and leapt to the ground near the food. While the animal ate, she stroked its back and noted that the collar was without inscription. The cat, as far as Martha was concerned, had no name and no owner.

After that it was easy to lure the creature into the house. She decided "Cat" was as good a name as any. She spoke to him in the same way that she had talked to Michael's essence in the empty space, except that now she had a visible focus for her one-sided conversation.

She didn't mind that the animal continued to ignore her, never even giving a sign that he heard her speaking to him. The arrangement was especially suitable because she could say anything she liked without fear of boring or annoying him. But, she decided, she would not attempt to put the question into words—to come right out and ask Cat if he had, in fact, devoured the bird that might have been the first posthumous manifestation of her husband. She was afraid he would answer—if only with a blink of his slanted, moon-colored eyes—and then she would know far too much.

# Mr. Sam

Mattie fanned herself with a pasteboard paddle fan. Streaks of perspiration ran down the back of her crumpled gray uniform. She could tolerate the late sundrenched afternoons on the roof-shaded porch of the nursing home, her ample body wedged into a wooden rocking chair, surrounded by her tranquil charges. What she didn't like was feeding and bathing the rusty old people, cleaning up their accidents.

"How come somebody don't give him a haircut? He reminds me of Saint Peter." Mattie's friend Estelle, who had stopped by on her way home from her housekeeping job, sat on the top step and regarded the frail, elderly man who maneuvered his wheelchair, an inch at the time, toward the edge of the long open porch.

"His daughter live in another state, don't ever come by but once every couple of months—she say leave him alone about his hair. He got himself a head full, don't he?" Mattie tapped Sam's shoulder sharply with the edge of her fan. She raised her voice: " 'Stelle want to know why you let your hair grow. She say you look like Saint Peter, but I say, you too mean to be Saint Peter. Maybe you Old Man Moses, he pretty tough. That who you is, Sam?" She shimmered with the satisfying knowledge that she could talk roughshod to a white man who still exuded authority, even though he was almost blind and, from the looks of him, almost dead.

"You better go while you can," he said urgently. "I'm warning you."

Mattie laughed, a rich sound that floated like the smell of warm sausage over the ancient people who stared at the sky with lackluster eyes, as if searching for signs of heaven. "You warning me, huh? Now, Sam, if I leave here, who gon' look after you dried-up old folks? You don't want Mattie to leave. I the one unzips your pants so you can pee."

Estelle said, in shocked appreciation, "You a mess, Mattie. Ought to be ashamed of yourself."

"Sam here, he the mess. Worst one we got. Always in a bad mood, growling like an old grizzly bear. The supervisor say he mad 'cause he ain't no big deal no more. She say those the ones hate most being put here."

Estelle said, noting his dark glasses, "I guess he's pretty near blind." She'd already assumed, since Mattie was talking so mean about him, that he was pretty near deaf.

Mattie said, "He got some idea that if his hair grow long enough, it make his eyesight come back strong. They get crazy notions here."

Estelle sighed, gathered up her large purse and umbrella. She wasn't going to stay around and listen to Mattie take out her ill humor on these helpless people any longer. It made her uncomfortable.

"Do you think it's about to storm?" A woman resident asked timidly as she peered at Estelle's umbrella.

"No ma'am, I carry this thing to hold off the sun," Estelle said, wishing she could explain to Mattie that the "ma'am" was in deference to the white woman's age.

Sam sat as straight as he could, his hands stretched out in front of him, as if searching for something to grasp. He cleared his throat, but his voice came out quavery and high-pitched. "When it's thundering, that means God is shouting, and you'd better listen."

Mattie rapped his shoulder again with her fan, harder than before. "What you talking about now, lunatic? A hellraiser like you don't know nothing whatsoever about God."

Estelle winced and said, as gently as she could to make up for Mattie's hatefulness, "Mr. Sam, I don't blame you for not cutting your pretty white hair. It's soft as a wool blanket."

"You'd better leave," he said as he turned his face toward her. His eyes were hidden by the opaque lenses of the glasses. "So you won't be here when it happens."

Mattie laughed, the sound as harsh as harmonica music. "Be quiet, old man. Ain't nothing going to happen 'round here, and I had enough of your raving for one day."

Estelle protested again. "We supposed to respect our elders, especially when they sick and pitiful and can't do for themselves."

Mattie snorted. "Go on home, girl. You sounding like some those white ladies breeze in here with church flowers on Sunday." The indignation that had been inside her for longer than she could remember erupted and she yelled, loud enough for the world to hear, "Old fools! Taking up space, when they ought to go on and die!"

Her words were still reverberating as Sam threw his hoard of strength into wresting the closest columns from their concrete roots. From the corner of her soul, Estelle saw it happen: the other columns snapped and toppled as if on cue; the roof and the walls caved in. But she had leapt over the shrubbery and was almost to the street when the final, earth-shaking crash came. The silence that followed was as peaceful as harp music. She glimpsed a wedge of white hair, splayed like the wing of an angel, beneath the devastation.

As she walked to the bus stop under the protection of her umbrella, Estelle felt acceptance settle on her like a shawl. Mr. Samson must have had his reasons this time around just as before. It didn't concern her. Anyway, she would never question the Bible, even if it repeated itself over and over and over, all the way to Judgment Day.

# Mourning

Tom ignored the question. After a short silence, Johnny spoke again. "Dad said you'd walk with me to my piano lesson since Mom has to stay for a meeting at the college today."

*Dad.* Why couldn't Johnny call him by his first name, as Tom did Kate? Tom was itching to clarify some things to his eight-year-old stepbrother, such as: "My dad is not your dad and your mom is okay, but she's not my mom, and as far as I'm concerned, you are merely a nuisance." Instead, after clearing his throat to make his voice sound more authoritative, he said, "Okay, but I don't plan to hang around and wait 'til you're through."

"Mom said she'd pick me up on her way home. But we ought to leave now. My lesson starts at four-thirty, and it's five after four."

"So it takes ten minutes at most." Tom sighed as he turned off his computer. "Come on, then." He put on his jacket. He wasn't going to remind the kid that it was still cool outside and he needed a sweater or something. It wasn't any skin off his nose if Johnny caught a cold and it turned into pneumonia.

Tom was determined that they would not walk together, or talk. The brisk March wind whipped at Johnny's thin, bare arms as he skipped along trying to keep up with Tom's pace.

The small cemetery in the middle of the next block hadn't been used for at least fifty years. The property was maintained—somewhat— by the town's historical society. Tom hadn't paid much attention to the place. At fourteen, he was too old for ghost stories, and he didn't have ties to anyone buried there. He and his dad had come to the town from a larger, busier city in another state the year before; his dad wanted Tom to have a wholesome environment with sidewalks, lawns big enough for ball games, and oak trees that umbrellaed the streets.

His dad had met Kate at the college where they both taught. A few months ago they were married, and Kate and Johnny, who was her only child, moved in, and Tom had been uncomfortable since. Not that there wasn't room in the large, older house that he and his dad had painted together. Tom had his own space, Johnny had his, and his dad and Kate had theirs. But they weren't a real family, and Tom missed the solidarity he'd had with his dad before Kate and Johnny came along—the three years they'd been by themselves after his mom had gone away. She had said Tom would be better off staying with his dad. She was busy with a demanding career.

"Here's the cemetery," Johnny said, as though he, Tom, didn't know one when he saw it. An iron fence, parallel to the sidewalk, was covered with curly ropes of dark, dusty ivy. "Have you ever been inside?"

"Sure," Tom said, although he hadn't.

"Want to cut through it now?"

"Okay," Tom said after a second's hesitation. He refastened the gate latch.

"We'll just follow this path," Johnny said.

"You act like we could get lost. It's not as though the place goes on for miles or anything. You can see clear through it to the other street."

"I know. I used to play in this cemetery when I was young."

"Young? What are you now?" Tom laughed. "Anyway, I don't believe you. You'd have been too scared to come in here by yourself."

"No, I wasn't. Mom thinks bad men might hang around here. That's why she's said I can't even walk past it anymore by myself," Johnny explained, "until I'm older. Probably next year."

Tom could see most of the cemetery without having to turn his head. "The only men in here are dead men."

"I wish my real dad was buried here," Johnny said, "instead of in Richmond, where we were living when he died. I used to come to one grave in here and pretend it was his."

"You're kidding."

"No, I'm not. Want to see which one?"

"Might as well." Tom followed as Johnny made his way past tombstones and thick solid shrubs before stopping at a plot with a single grave.

Johnny said, "This man's all by himself, so I figured he didn't have any family, and I could borrow him. Especially since his name was Walter, same as my father's."

Tom stooped to read the inscription on the granite stone. "But this guy was born in 1870 and died in 1925. And his name was Walter Brown. Your last name is Carson."

"I just pretended he was my dad," Johnny said softly. "Anyway, now that I have a new dad, I don't need to talk to this Walter."

A *new dad.* Tom felt his face flush. With his foot, he nudged a crockery mug that was propped against the tombstone. "Wonder where this came from?" he said.

"I used to put flowers in it." Johnny picked up the mug and brushed dirt from it. He moved a few feet away, to a flat marker that retained some of its original whiteness. Tom didn't have to stoop to read the words etched in large, grayed script: "Martha Sturdivant, Beloved Mother" and the dates: "1867–1932."

Johnny scooped up a handful of wild violets from a nearby patch, put them in the mug and filled it with water from a ground faucet. He placed it at the head of the slab of marble that ran the length and width of Martha Sturdivant's grave. "She's by herself, too." He looked at Tom, took a breath before continuing: "I know your real mom's name is Martha. So maybe sometimes, when you need to feel close to her, you could talk to this Martha."

My mother's not dead, she's in California. Tom opened his mouth to say those words, but didn't. They wouldn't answer the question Johnny had asked him earlier, the question he had pretended not to hear: "Do you miss your mother?"

Tom would never do it, but suddenly he could imagine how it would be to lie face down on the marble and mourn the loss of her, letting his tears fill the carved-out niches of the words Beloved Mother. He would feel the hard smoothness through his clothes, through his skin, until his bones connected with the cool stone. He let his eyes meet Johnny's. "Thanks for the suggestion," he said lightly. "I'll keep it in mind."

Tom took off his jacket and put it around the younger boy's shoulders. "Better wear this. You could catch cold and first thing you know the whole family would have it—you, me, Dad, Kate." He shrugged off the gratitude offered in Johnny's quick grin.

They emerged from the gate on the other side of the cemetery. The music teacher's house was directly across the street. Tom watched from the curb until Johnny had gone through the front door. Then he ran, leaping across the lines of the sidewalk, his shoulders hunched against the chill, as he took the long way home.

# Harmonious Arrangement

The Christmas tree, a convincing replica of Scotch pine, stood like an upright corpse in a corner of the dining room. Ornaments nestled in quiet profusion among pliant evergreen branches. A *papier-mâché* angel presided over the conical symmetry with an expression of serene goodwill. Lily had unplugged the labyrinth of miniature lights; otherwise she hadn't touched the tree since Christmas day. It was well into March, and the children were embarrassed.

"It's asinine," Susan said, using the word for perhaps the first time in her life. She was twelve, and not nearly as beautiful in body or spirit as her brother. Lily knew that "asinine" would be her word of the week.

Sure enough: "Really asinine," Susan repeated with emphasis and the ring of confidence in her voice. "Agnes nearly flipped when she saw the thing. She said leaving a Christmas tree up past New Year's Day is in bad taste. It makes us look weird." Agnes was Susan's

idol, not yet a firm friend, who had visited after school that afternoon.

"I know you're trying to make a point, Mom, but what is it?" said James, who was fifteen, and Lily's heart. She would have gone through fire for him. Why wouldn't she take down the Christmas tree? At first it was a little in-family joke. So they thought, James and Susan and their father, Lily's husband Edgar, who was preoccupied with his world outside the realm of the home, and inclined to humor Lily and the children as long as possible about most things.

They were having dinner. The subject of the conversation was hardly intrusive, Lily thought, gazing across the table to where the tree cowered in its corner—No, it didn't cower, it simply filled a space. If it had been a china cabinet in similar desuetude, full of unused dishes and tarnished silver, the children wouldn't have made an issue of it. The truth was, she had tired of the annual production involved in setting up and, especially, taking down the tree. Fragile ornaments had to be put away in eggcrate boxes, the branches disassembled and regrouped according to color code, and more than a dozen strings of lights had to be separated and recoiled individually. Each year it was Lily who climbed up into the airless loft—ghosts were there, she knew it, even though the house wasn't old enough to have them—and brought the boxes down one by one. The tree itself had a sturdy cardboard container, almost coffin-sized, with compartments for its limbs and sections of trunk.

Making the tree into a thing of splendor in mid December always seemed to take a day of her life: most of the morning, counting interruptions, just to put the sections together—she wasn't mathematical or particularly dexterous—and half an afternoon to ply it with decoration. She had made the treetop angel herself in a crafts class some years before where she learned, as she had suspected, that she was creative only in a broad sense. Nevertheless, she was rather proud of her angel—the suggestion of features on a trusting face, the gentle lift of graceful wings. She had brushed on extra coats of lacquer until it was as glossy and solid as porcelain.

She had bought the artificial tree at least five years before, after coming to the conclusion that blue-green pines severed from their roots tended not to last through the holiday season. It didn't take long to talk herself into the purchase. She visualized a frosty forest where the tree might have thrived, unsuspecting, before it was chopped down and transported cross-country on a truck (had it been real, instead of manufactured in Hong Kong).

It was a sensible decision, she thought, to replace a dying, mutilated tree with a facsimile that would never shed its needles onto the carpet, never end up in a bonfire. The neighborhood had an annual party just before New Year's where the men dragged browning pines and cedars, still dripping bits of tinsel, to a vacant lot at the end of the block. With ceremony, someone set the pile ablaze. Families watched the conflagration while they drank hot chocolate and rum toddies and tried to find things to laugh about. Lily imagined she could hear faint cries of dryads consumed by smoke and flame. She thought Christmas shouldn't be finished with forced camaraderie and paganistic ritual. As far as the family was concerned, the transition from real to fake tree had been smooth enough. Edgar was relieved not to have to haul a dead tree to the party each year, and the children simply continued to go anyway.

"It has been in that spot for almost three months and you've hardly noticed it. Next December, we'll plug in the lights and it will become the center of attention again," Lily said. She pulled a leaf from her artichoke and dipped it into mayonnaise, which she hadn't made from scratch, but had spooned from a jar.

"What's after these yuck things?" Susan had not touched her artichoke. Edgar was attacking his as though it were a chore to be finished. Only James obviously relished each mouthful, which was why she had served them.

"Beef-a-noodle," Lily admitted.

"That doesn't go with artichokes," James said, his face slack with disappointment. "Why do you make us think we're having this really gourmet meal with the first course and then fade into canned crap for the main dish?"

"I planned to cook a roast, but I didn't have time. I had to show a house."

"Big deal," James said. "When are you going to sell one of those houses you show?"

Edgar was slicing the artichoke heart into small, neat pieces on his plate. A pile of gnawed leaves leaned precariously over the edge of it.

"Don't belittle your mother's efforts to establish a career for herself," he said. "I'm counting on her. It's time we became a two-income family. Otherwise you may not go to college." He was not being serious. Edgar was a successful certified public accountant, and it was a foregone conclusion that James would qualify for a merit scholarship.

Susan tossed the artichoke from one hand to another like a tennis ball.

"Agnes's mother is an attorney. But she only works part-time three days a week."

"And the other two days she plays bridge full time," Lily said, but she was guessing. She didn't know Agnes's mother.

"What's wrong with that?" Susan looked alarmed.

"It's decadent," James said. Darling James. "I'm glad Mom doesn't play bridge. It's sort of like being an alcoholic."

"Son, you don't know what you're talking about.

Bridge is a game for intellectuals. That's why your mother never took to it." Edgar stabbed the last wedge of the silvery green heart, gave it a thorough dunking in his sauce cup, and waved it for emphasis on the way to his mouth.

"You really are insufferable sometimes, Edgar," Lily said. "Most of the time," she amended.

Susan's cry was pure anguish. "Please don't talk to Daddy like that! I'm afraid you'll do it in front of my friends. I would die if you did."

"I'll try to remember not to, then." Lily took her own plate of artichoke waste to the kitchen. The canned pasta, simmering in a pan on the stove, gave off a slight odor of scorch. She scooped and scraped it into a dish, emptied half a jar of parmesan cheese over it. She could hear their voices from the dining room. They were back on the subject of the Christmas tree.

"You should flat tell her it's got to go, Dad." James, traitor!

Edgar's voice was smooth. "By leaving the thing there, she's making a statement. Like she does all the work around here and nobody helps. Housework is menial, and your mother never has taken to it in the least. Yet, she never wanted the responsibility of delegating work to a part-time maid, which I have repeatedly offered her, and she didn't train you two to help out around the house."

"She never lets us decorate the tree, either," Susan

said. "She always does it by herself while we're at school."

"That's because she wants it to be perfect," James said. "And when we were little we messed it up."

"Why does she want it to be perfect when nothing else around here is?" Susan asked.

"Good point," Edgar said. (Lily, still poised beyond the doorway, knew he was nodding his head.) "She's never been a perfectionist about anything that I know of. However, I suggest you stop criticizing and take the plates to the kitchen." He looked up as Lily came in and placed the casserole in front of him. He smiled. "Ah, the beef-a-whatever. It does smell interesting."

"At least it has cheese on it," James said. Lily went back to the kitchen and returned with a basket of rolls and fresh plates.

"That's it?" Susan looked from the casserole to the bread.

"That's it, take it or leave it," Lily said grimly, reseating herself. Edgar had begun to serve the plates.

"I'm never ever going to ask Agnes to spend the night with me," Susan said, "unless you promise me we'll have something decent for supper."

"At least she uses the sterling silver all the time," James said. "I'll bet your dumb Agnes's mom never uses anything but stainless steel."

"They have a maid who serves their dinner," Susan said.

Lily went over to the tree. She stretched to lift the angel from the top and dropped it in her skirt pocket, savoring for a moment a swift memory of her hands as they kneaded the creature into being. "That's all I want to save," she said. "You may take the rest of the stuff off and throw it away or put it somewhere. I really don't care."

The realization that she really didn't care was like a breath of clean air, but still she fled to the kitchen. She could hear them, hear the efficient rustle of teamwork as they set about stripping the tree. Edgar and James and Susan dropped things, clinking and jangling, some-times shattering, into grocery sacks. After she had loaded the dishwasher, Lily went out and sat alone on the patio, shivering in the dry March wind. In less than ten minutes, they had denuded the plastic tree; like phantoms, their shadowy shapes emerged from the house dragging the unresisting carcass, its branches swishing like broomstraw across the pavement of the driveway. Edgar and James and Susan pulled the limbs from their sockets, broke the trunk down into sections, and crammed all the pieces into the large rubbish container behind the garage. Edgar fastened the lid on firmly with a resounding snap. He would see to it that James put the container on the curb for pickup.

The sacks of adornment were shoved into a closet.

It wasn't until the next morning, when Lily took a load of clothes from the dryer and discovered that the lump in a pocket of her denim skirt was not a wad of tissues, that she wept. Redefined by the washer's agitator and the heat of the dryer, the angel lay like a small wounded bird in her hands; the waterlogged wings drooped with a forlornness she could feel in her bones, and the face was a tiny, twisted oval of shock.

# Monday

Myra awoke with a headache that throbbed as intensely as a love song on MTV. The analogy came as she pulled herself from the clutches of the last dream, and she thought, I should write that down before I forget it; I might want to use it in the novel. But she wouldn't. She had never got in the habit of keeping notepad and pencil handy.

She was washing down Tylenol with tepid water from the bathroom faucet when Sharon called from the direction of the kitchen: "Mom, please get up. I don't want to be late for school."

Sharon would have coffee started, juice poured, cereal waiting in bowls on the breakfast table. For eight years old, she was maddeningly efficient.

"Have I ever failed to get you to school on time?" Myra noticed the morning newspaper neatly folded by her place mat, and added, "Never mind answering that." She hugged Sharon. The frail, small body stiffened against the rough texture of Myra's robe. "What's the matter, Bird-bones? Getting too big for a hug from your best friend in the world?"

"You smell like wine," Sharon said. "I saw the empty bottle in the garbage."

"Well, that's not any big deal. There was less than half a bottle to begin with. Not even a cupful." As Myra sprinkled sugar over her cereal, her hand shook, causing the spoon to jiggle more than was necessary to get the job done. She was prepared to make a joke of it, but Sharon pretended not to notice. The headache was still banging away. "Sweetie, would you get me a cup of coffee?"

Sharon had anticipated her and was pouring coffee into a mug. "Daddy and Kay drink Scotch and water," she said. "Kay never has but one drink. Then she makes dinner while Daddy has his second. And they never drink after dinner."

Daddy and Kay. If she didn't have a headache already, the mention of her ex-husband and his new wife would trigger one. The counselor had cautioned her never to make disparaging remarks about them. Myra counted to three silently, then said, "Your daddy and Kay are really rather dull people. Now forget I said that. Poof! It's gone, isn't it?" She laughed, hoping to coax Sharon into a smile. When it wasn't forthcoming, she added irritably, "I'm not my usual long-suffering self this morning, so I will point out one more thing. I have to settle for grocery store wine. I can't afford good Scotch."

No. She would not start off a new week being caustic to her only child. Sharon loved her. No matter how full of fun and games those structured visits with Daddy and Kay were, Sharon's bond with her mother was strong and sure. "Take your new sweater. It's supposed to turn cool today," Myra said.

Sharon rinsed her bowl, then placed it in the dishwasher before she said, "You mean the sweater Kay gave me?"

"No, the red sweater I bought you."

"Oh," Sharon said. "That one."

"Yes indeed, that one." Daddy and Kay had lucrative careers and no babies yet. Myra wished Kay wouldn't shop for Sharon at all. As long as the child support payments kept coming, she could clothe Sharon without additional help from them.

Myra put on a warm-up suit and tennis shoes, brushed her hair, splashed water on her face. The headache was letting up; her hands had stopped shaking. It was Monday morning, the week-end was past, she was in control. As soon as she returned from driving Sharon to school, she'd get right to work. First, the ad copy. Boring, predictable, but bread-and-butter. Then she would start on the brochure for the Historical Society. That was a plum, a challenge she would enjoy.

Since she'd been freelancing—the public relations

job hadn't worked out—she had more time for her own writing. The novel, which was about a divorcée not unlike herself, got off to a good start, but she hadn't given much time to it lately. An advertising agency had just given her a trial month on a weekly real estate ad column. Before her cash settlement from the divorce got dangerously low, she'd be earning more. "Now who's holding us up?" She called down the hall toward Sharon's room.

At the school, Sharon kissed Myra's cheek, as she did each morning before getting out of the car. "See you this afternoon, Mom," she said, gamefully trying not to make it a question.

Myra reassured her. "Your chauffeur in the Toyota that's as old as you are will be right here at three-fifteen."

Sharon whispered—as though embarrassed that someone might hear—"I get scared when you're late. I think you might have had a wreck."

"You worry too much. Stop it, you hear? Have a good day, chicken." As Myra drove home, she determined to have a good, productive day herself.

She had straightened the kitchen and started the washing machine when she looked out the window and saw some old-fashioned-looking roses climbing over the fence from a neighbor's yard. She rummaged in a drawer, found scissors, and went out to clip a few that were on her side of the fence. She put the roses in a vase, admiring the way they fell into artful arrangement without any effort on her part, as words did when the writing was going well. Sometimes—a lot of the time, in fact—her life fell into some semblance of artful arrangement without her doing much about it, one way or the other.

By half past nine, she was producing mechanical prose on the word processor screen. "3 BR contemporary, charm and efficiency combined. Desirable neighborhood with trees and sidewalks." [Don't give the exact location, and don't mention that there's only one bath.] The wind-up: "Super financing. Priced to sell!" Next: "For the up-and-coming executive, stately Georgian with gorgeous landscaping, private study for Dad, cozy sewing room for Mom. Just listed, bargain of the week. Call now—this one won't stay on the market long!" Before noon, she had composed the week's quota of thirty ads, each with the requisite adjectives and exclamation points. She would take the copy to the agency on the way to pick up Sharon.

She opened the refrigerator to get mayonnaise to mix with a can of tuna. An emerald-green bottle of vermouth, left by someone who took his gin home with him, gleamed at her from the refrigerator door rack. She didn't care for vermouth—it tasted like strong perfume smelled. But she might have an ounce or two on the rocks before she made her sandwich.

She pulled out a chair, sat down at the table, and

placed the bottle beside the vase of roses. The glass of ice cubes in her hand was a promise of warmth to follow. She would use this time to relax, but also to take stock, to redefine her goals. Sharon's well-being was her foremost priority. She would make a special supper for the two of them: Stroganoff, salad, and chocolate mousse (which Sharon still called chocolate mouse). She would use the good china. Long-ranging resolutions ticked through her mind as though it were New Year's Eve. She would be a better mother, keep the house neat and clean, get her copywriting work done ahead of schedule, and spend at least three hours each day on the novel.

Myra sipped the cool, slippery liquid that warmed her clear to her toes and felt tears on her cheeks as she thought of her precious, beautiful, sensitive little girl. She wasn't going to let them—her sanctimonious ex-husband and that calculating what's-her-name—take her baby away. Sharon would never leave her mother. They knew that. Didn't they?

She was clutching the empty bottle when the phone rang. She raised her head from where it had settled, heavy as a pumpkin, on the table. Her shoulders ached from being hunched over her arms. A woman's voice, crisply hostile, informed her that her daughter was waiting at the school. It was four-fifteen.

Myra heard herself glibly assure the woman that she was on her way. "Time seems to evaporate when I'm working on deadline. I'm really sorry. I'll leave right now."

She heard the woman's sigh (of exasperation, disapproval, contempt?) and added, her voice surging with the conviction of her heart and mind, "My daughter knows she comes first—Sharon knows she can count on me."

But there was a definite click on the other end of the line before she got that last part out.

# Seventeen Times
# As High As The Moon

L ike a hen come to roost, the alien presence on her balding head was settled in, already making itself at home. Jess had not chosen camouflage in the gray-brown range of her own hair color. The improbable shade of silver was a gesture of defiance to the lion inside her body: after six blasts of chemotherapy, the beast was temporarily stunned. From anyone but Alice, her five-year-old neighbor from the house next door, the compliment just paid—"Your new wig is really and truly the most gorgeous thing I've ever seen"—would sound like fakery acknowledging fakery.

"Thank you. I hoped you would approve," Jess said. "Why are we whispering?"

"Mama told me not to mention one word about it. So I didn't mention, I whispered." Alice had resumed her normal voice, which was always tinged with excitement, curiosity, or wonder. "It makes you look like somebody else. Bet you can't guess who."

"Well, let's see. One of the Marx Brothers wore a headpiece, as I recall. Was it Groucho?"

"Groucho?" Alice giggled, then frowned. "I wouldn't answer if somebody called me that. Why didn't he change his name to something nicer?"

"He probably was given a perfectly good name, but the stage name helped make his image as a movie star." Jess felt defensive when Alice questioned the ways of the world.

"Anyway, the person I'm thinking about isn't a movie star, she's in the nursery rhyme book."

Jess poured more tea into Alice's cup. They had agreed early on that lemonade shouldn't be served at real tea parties. "So now I look like Mother Goose?"

"Not *her*, she's pretty much of a haggard." Alice's disdain received the same exaggeration as her enthusiasm. "You look like that lady who sweeps up the sky."

"Show her to me." The book of nursery rhymes on the coffee table was a leftover from the childhood of Jess's only son, Robert, who lived halfway across the country with his wife and two almost-grown boys. Robert thought she should relocate to that place, to be close to them, her only family. Twelve years before, when she was first alone and still sound of body, such a move had not been suggested. Now she could not bear the thought of being uprooted. She didn't try to explain to him that the house and town she'd lived in for fifty years tethered her, kept her bound to the earth like a long standing tree. She had dependable friends who came around, despite their embarrassment at having their own health. Best of all, for short, sweet visits two or three afternoons a week she had Alice, who treated her as though she were fully dimensional and not some transparent half-ghost.

Alice had found the page she was looking for. "Here she is."

Jess studied the illustration. The artist had sketched a graceful acquiescence into the figure of a white-haired, serenely countenanced woman who leaned into the clouds from an airborne basket.

"Is seventeen times as high as the moon as far away as that town in Ohio where your son lives?" Alice asked.

"Even farther."

They were sitting side by side on the sofa. Alice wiped cookie crumbs from her chin and said, "Will you read it to me?"

"I thought you'd never ask." Jess read in the measured sing-song chant the child expected:

*There was an old woman tossed in a blanket*
*Seventeen times as high as the moon*
*But where she was going no mortal could tell*
*For under her arm she carried a broom.*
*"Old woman, old woman, old woman," said I*

*"Whither, oh whither, oh whither so high?"*
*"To sweep the cobwebs from the sky*
*"And I'll be with you bye and bye."*

Alice had chimed in softly toward the end. After a moment of silent foot-swinging she said, "Jess, what's a mortal?"

"A somebody. I'm one, you're one."

"Can dead people be mortals?" She was whispering again.

"No, but sometimes they get to be immortal. That means they live on as memories in the minds of others." Trite, too preachy, and much more than she meant to say.

But Alice regarded her in rapt admiration, as she had on a previous occasion when she marveled at the veins in Jess's hands: "They're so big and purple"; or the time she informed her, "You're not one bit old in dog years." Now she said, stringing the words out like pearls, "I'll remember you forever."

Jess sighed. From the first, their rapport had been based on truth and, occasionally, on pleasantly profound absurdity. A few minutes with Alice was like skipping rope again. It was the closest she'd come to knowing what it might have been like to have a child or grandchild of her own gender—but it wasn't supposed to get cumbersome. Alice belonged to others. "I'll remember you, too, when I'm sweeping cobwebs in the sky." In her diminished voice, the words came out lightly, as she'd meant them to.

"Do you really think you can just hang around up there after you—" Alice stopped; the unspoken filled the air like swirls of dust particles.

"I have absolutely no idea what will be required of me." How would she handle the ultimate exit? Would she—could she—move from one plane to another in graceful acquiescence? Jess wanted very much, at that moment, to close her eyes and place her head, the part of her that was already enshrouded, against the back of the sofa.

"Now see here, Jess—you can't *die*!" Alice spat the word out like a wad of gum that had lost its flavor. She threw her arms around Jess's neck; after the brief hug, she walked quickly to the front door. Before she let herself out, she turned to say firmly, "But even if you do, I will pretend you didn't."

"In that event, I'll sure enough be immortal." Jess gave a smile as good as the one she got.

Twilight as purple as her veins had filled the windows when the phone's ringing roused her from a state of semi-sleep, which was one of the better by-products of the illness and its treatment.

"Mother?" Robert always managed to put duty, preoccupation, resentment, and love into his querulous one-word greeting.

The only way not to let Alice down completely

would be to disappear, in one fell swoop, while still in reasonably good shape. Jess said, into the phone, "I'm ready to relocate—the sooner the better—if you still want me to come."

Robert assured her he would take care of everything: "The move will not be hard on you."

Spoken across the distance, the perfunctory words took on the glow of prophecy; she felt as though a hand had been placed on her head in blessing.

# Saints

You leave a place, and years later, you suddenly start to think about it again—especially the people there who taught you something about life. I'm remembering my Uncle Potter and an attractive widow who owned Magdalene's Beauty Parlor in the town where I spent most of my childhood.

"Hey, hon," Lena would say, looking up from shampooing someone's head to beam at me when we went in on Thursday afternoons for my mother's standing appointment. The fumes from the permanent wave developer made my eyes sting, but I liked the pink and purple wallpaper and the cheerful atmosphere. Especially, I liked Lena, which is what everyone called her. We never even thought about her real name being Magdalene. "I got a brand new *Motion Picture Magazine* around here somewhere . . . and you can get yourself a Coke out of the ice box whenever you feel like it," she'd say as I settled down to wait out the hour it took for my mother to get shampooed, set, and combed out. Lena was her own best advertisement, with her hair bleached to the color of honeysuckle and arranged in whatever she thought was the latest style.

Uncle Potter wasn't my blood uncle, but my Aunt Gertrude's husband. They were old enough to be my grandparents, which I didn't have, and childless themselves, they took a kind interest in me. He was head of the English department at the small liberal arts college and a staunch deacon in the First Baptist Church. From his pew down front, he would interject an occasional firm "Amen" after some point was made in the Sunday sermon. He kept a notebook discreetly handy for recording the preacher's grammatical errors. These he would go over with the man during the following week. I had encountered the preacher when he came to Uncle Potter's house for improvement sessions—I went there frequently myself to practice on the Baldwin spinet— but I was surprised to open the front door one day to the preacher's wife, who asked, through tight lips, to see my uncle. After I had taken her to his study I put my ear to the wall to eavesdrop.

She got right to the purpose of her visit. "Dr. Potter, it appears my husband has got himself involved with that woman who runs the beauty parlor downtown. Lena Tanton."

Uncle Potter was clearly surprised. "Have you confronted him with this charge?"

"No, sir, he's still out of town at the state convention, and won't be back until the end of the week. I just learned of this sorry business through an unsigned letter." Mrs. Jackson's voice trembled with righteousness. "That hussy is not even a member of his flock."

Uncle Potter thanked Mrs. Jackson for confiding in him, and assured her he would look into the matter. He told her he was not inclined to put much stock in a malicious rumor from an anonymous source. But Mrs. Jackson left as agitated as she was when she arrived.

I could hardly wait to go to the beauty parlor with my mother the next day. I wanted to see if Lena looked any different now that I had heard she might be a home breaker and a hussy. I had read about women who took other women's husbands in *True Confessions*. In fact, the only place I had access to that magazine was in Magdalene's Beauty Parlor. I thought with pure admiration that Lena certainly did look the part: her eyebrows were thinned almost to non-existence, arched like half-moons, and penciled black. The color on her cheeks matched the traffic light red on her mouth. Her green eyes looked excited even when she wasn't, and she had mountainous breasts that floated when she walked. I was staring at her, but she didn't appear to notice. She kept up a steady stream of chatter as she always did. "You're so lucky, Mrs. Carter," she said. "You're gonna go gray in the prettiest way. Just salt and pepper. None of them ugly yellowish streaks."

That wasn't what my mother wanted to hear. "I'm not going to go gray," she said. "I want you to start dying it soon as I get too many to pluck."

Lena sighed and shifted gum from one side of her mouth to the other. "Sugar, it would go against my principles. We'd have to use black dye, and it would be too harsh looking on you."

It occurred to me then that she was as sincere in her way as the Baptist preacher was in his way, and another thing they had in common was their lapses in speaking good English, although the Baptist preacher's lapses weren't quite of the scope of Lena's.

Lena rotated my mother's scalp in rhythmic swirls of lather while she talked. The other operators, Betty Sue and Nell, chatted with their own customers as they worked on their heads. The long narrow room, with three porcelain sinks in a linoleum-covered counter against one wall and three big-hooded hair dryers lined up against another, seemed both cozy and exotic. That day, as I sat by myself on a plastic-covered loveseat near the entrance, reading about Lana Turner, I was the first to see Mrs. Jackson. She appeared disoriented, as though she'd never been inside such an establishment before; if that was the case, the permanent wave machine alone could have scared the wits out of her. But she wasn't scareable, she was determined. As soon as she got her bearings, she headed toward Lena, who was intent on her ministrations to my mother, who was swathed in oilcloth up to her chin and laid back in a tilting chair with her head hanging over the sink. "Adulteress!" Mrs. Jackson said, in a timid voice, as though she were trying out the word for the first time.

Lena's expression did not change. "I beg your pardon?" she said coolly. She wiped her hands on a towel and placed them on her hips as she continued to speak very slowly, enunciating each syllable with precision. "Was you speaking to me, madam?"

My mother struggled to an upright position. I could tell in a flash she'd heard the gossip. Her mouth fell open, but she closed it, wisely. I was right by the telephone; I picked it up and gave the operator Uncle Potter's number, praying he'd be home, which was in the first block past downtown. When he answered I said, quietly but importantly, "The preacher's wife is making a scene in Magdalene's." The rhyme was accidental, but I laughed from nervousness. "You'd better come on over here." I hung up without waiting for his response, because I didn't want to miss anything. My mother had eased herself out of the chair and looked as though she might make a dash toward the door. She may have forgotten I was there. Betty Sue and Nell moved in to flank Lena. The other women, with their heads soaking wet or helmeted with rows of curlers, scurried silently toward the front of the shop where I was, then turned to watch the action.

Now that she had an audience, Mrs. Jackson overcame all timidity. She said in full voice, "You may not know the word of God, but you cannot deny you know the meaning of the word *adultery*."

Lena cocked her magnificent head to one side and looked the woman up and down before she spoke. She could have played Medea at that moment. "What does God think about crazy women like you who don't know what the hell they're talking about? Tell me that, sister." The custom was to call the preacher "brother" and his wife "sister" but I didn't think Lena meant "sister" in that sense. Mrs. Jackson was probably right in assuming Lena didn't know the word of God, because even though Lena was proud of her name coming from the Bible, she didn't attend any church. I had heard her tell my mother once that she stood on her feet every day in the week and Sunday was the only day she could get off them. It seemed to me that it would be pretty near impossible for her and the Reverend Jackson to get together, since his main work day was Sunday and she had to work all the other days.

Mrs. Jackson said, "I had to see you for myself." She nodded her head as though she approved of what she saw: "I figured you'd be all painted up." At that remark, the other women all looked in the wall mirrors; every face there but mine and Mrs. Jackson's had some degree of artifice on it. But Lena really was painted *up*. When she smiled her face cracked through a vanilla-colored glaze; each of her eyelashes held a tiny bead of soot. I thought the effect was wonderful. Mrs. Jackson's eyelashes were so pale she might as well not have had any. I was on Lena's side.

"If you're finished with your insults, kindly leave my place of business," Lena said, framing each word with her mouth as though Mrs. Jackson had to lip-read. She began to file her nails, as though she were bored. If she thought the steam was out of the other woman, she had misjudged the situation. Mrs. Jackson picked up a pitcher of water, which was there for rinsing hair, and threw the contents at Lena's surprised face. Gasps of shock came from the onlookers, me included. At that moment in strode Uncle Potter on what undoubtedly was his first visit to Magdalene's Beauty Parlor, too.

"Ladies, this will not do, please calm yourselves," he said sternly as he placed himself between Mrs. Jackson and Lena.

Lena glared at him. "She busted in here without an appointment and called me an unmentionable name. Then she threw a pitcher of my own water in my face. Dr. Potter, I'm gonna wade into her, so you'd better move outa my way." She rubbed her hands together as if she were a prizefighter.

But Uncle Potter didn't budge. He said, "This controversy should be settled in private, Magdalene."

Mrs. Jackson said, "You mean her name really is Magdalene? Well, if that isn't fitting—she's named for the worst sinner in the New Testament."

Poor Lena. She whirled around toward Uncle Potter, who stood immovable as a tree between them, his rimless spectacles about to slide off his nose. "Is that true?"

Uncle Potter said, loud enough for everybody there to hear, "You are named for one of the best friends our Savior ever had, and you, Mrs. Jackson, are blaspheming a saint." Then he said quietly, "Only she who is blameless should cast the first stone. Examine yourself, my dear, and see if you are lacking in ways that may have caused strain in your marriage."

I was so proud of him, I wanted to go and bury my face against his bony chest, but since I had never been that demonstrative with him before, I didn't. Mrs. Jackson sort of folded up after that. She put her hands up to her face and cried softly, and Uncle Potter escorted her out of the shop, speaking gently to her as he did so. He came back in, waited until he had everyone's attention, then said, "Talking about this incident would not serve any useful purpose whatsoever." The women looked at each other and tried not to smile.

Lena had dried her face, smoothed herself back into shape. She tilted her chin to show she still had her pride. "Dr. Potter," she said, as she walked with him to the door, low enough so the others wouldn't hear, "Was Mary Magdalene really one of the best friends Jesus ever had?"

Uncle Potter said, "Yes, indeed. She was a great

comfort to Him." And then he added, "I suggest you not think about Mrs. Jackson or her husband. Put your mind, instead, on noble thoughts. As you are named for one of the Good Book's saints, you owe it to yourself to learn more about the Bible. Toward that end I invite you to attend the adult Sunday School class I teach at the First Baptist Church. Not right away, but say in about a month." With that, he tipped his hat to include everybody and beckoned me to come outside with him. "You did right to call me," he said and gave me a quarter.

Within the month, the Reverend Jackson got a call to a church in the other end of the state. (Before they moved, Mrs. Jackson went to the only other beauty parlor in town and got a manicure and a permanent wave.) By the time his resignation was announced, a committee headed by Uncle Potter had found a replacement, a young man just out of seminary, who spoke good English. Uncle Potter would sit in church with pen poised above the little notepad on his knee, but he soon realized he wouldn't need those things any more. I imagine he missed his weekly tutorials with the Reverend Jackson. After the talk had died down, which it always did in a town that size as soon as there was some new scandal to take its place, Lena started coming to Uncle Potter's Sunday School class. She would sit next to Aunt Gertrude, who smiled at her as though they were best friends. All of Aunt Gertrude's friends were of a type, however—members of the Women's Christian Temperance Union who didn't even play bridge.

As the town grew, Lena enlarged her beauty business. She hired more girls, had booths put in "for privacy" (despite the partitions, you still could hear everything), and installed a new sign with MARY MAGDALENE'S HOUSE OF BEAUTY spelled out in bright-colored neon tubes. Her makeup became more subdued, but she kept her hair the color of honeysuckle.

The last time I saw her was over twenty years later, at Uncle Potter's funeral. (We had moved to another state when I was in junior high school. I could count on one hand the times I was around Uncle Potter from the time we left until he died.) I found Lena as the group at the cemetery began to disperse. "Remember me?" I asked her. "I used to come with my mother to your shop and read your movie mags."

"Sure I do, hon," she said, giving me a hug. "I remember it was you, had to be, who called Dr. Potter to come get that crazy woman off me. Actually, you had a lot to do with my salvation."

"I'm glad," I said, with disappointment. I had never thought it was true about her and the Reverend Jackson. "Did you ever marry again, Lena?"

"Yes, I did, God rest his soul. I had several years of good life with a man who was a widower when we met. Despite what they used to say about me, I never wanted to take any man away from his wife." She continued, "After your uncle explained to me about my name, I decided to try to live up to it." She smiled with such triumph that I basked in the warmth of it. "I'll tell you something else," she said. "Since Dr. Potter turned my life around, I don't go by Lena anymore. I answer to my full Christian name. Everybody calls me Mary Magdalene."

Driving away from the town that day, I tried to recall something from the funeral eulogy that I could relate to my own feelings about Uncle Potter. Finally I had it. Somewhere in that rambling oratory filled with scripture and platitudes, the man had said, "George Potter was never touched by scandal, dishonesty, or any of the sheer meanness which surrounds us on this earth. He was above it all, as few men are."

"Amen." Even though there was no one to hear me, I said it aloud.